MY FATHER'S HOUSE

2

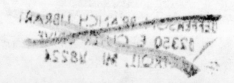

MY FATHER'S HOUSE

DIJORN MOSS

URBAN
CHRISTIAN

www.urbanchristianonline.net

Urban Books
1199 Straight Path
West Babylon, NY 11704

My Father's House © copyright 2008 Dijorn Moss

ISBN-13: 978-1-60162-970-8
ISBN-10: 1-60162-970-2

First Printing October 2008
Printed in the United States of America

10   9   8   7   6   5   4   3   2   1

*This is a work of fiction. Any references or similarities to actual events, real
people, living, or dead, or to real locales are intended to give the novel a sense
of reality. Any similarity in other names, characters, places, and incidents is
entirely coincidental.*

Distributed by Kensington Corp.
Submit Wholesale Orders to:
Kensington Publishing Corp.
C/O Penguin Group (USA) Inc.
Attention: Order Processing
405 Murray Hill Parkway
East Rutherford, NJ 07073-2316
Phone: 1-800-526-0275
Fax: 1-800-227-9604

Dedications

To my wife, Trinea,
A virtuous woman who I will gladly spend my life bringing
her the treasures of the world.

&

To Pastor Oscar Dace
Great pastor. Great mentor. Great friend.

Acknowledgments

This journey was made possible by God and the many people He sent along the way to help guide me to this first book. I do not believe in chance, but I believe in purpose, and for that, I acknowledge God and my Lord and Savior Jesus Christ. Thank you for believing in me when I did not believe in myself, and whenever I heard that my dreams were impossible, you whispered to me that they were possible. Thank you for forgiving my sins and not allowing my past to impede on my future.

To my mother, who worked rotating shifts to provide for my sister and me. Thank you, Mom, for your love and sacrifice. To my father, who pushed me to give my best in everything and not make excuses. Thank you for being a role model and a father. To my sister, Rashilda, for being a strong black woman who gave birth to my two precious nephews, Anthony and Aaron. To my stepmother, Elianna, stepfather, David, and my in-laws, Johnnie and Trina Kizzie, thank you guys for your love and support over the years. To my grandmother, Ruth Jonice, who personifies strength. To the English teacher who changed my life, Iris. Thank you for reading me those poems. They sparked a desire to write and change the world with my words.

To my mentors, Scott Sublett and Ethel Walker, thank you for teaching me the principles of dramatic writing and for giving me opportunities to have my voice heard. To the many teachers who played vital roles in my development: Genelle Austin-Lett, Mr. Porvechio, Dr. Linda Mitchell, Dr. Samuel Miao, Erma Jackson, Professor Bob Dickerson, Dr. Steven Millner, and Dr. Jill Stienberg, thank you for imparting your wisdom and guidance. To the brilliant Floyd Salas, my life will never be the same after taking your novel writing course.

To my closest friends: Mike Jacques, Jaton Gunter, Deacon Mike Boykins, Quinn Taylor, and the rest of the domino clique. My college memories are priceless, and I thank you guys for your love and support. To Mike Garret and Steve Kimball, your friendships have truly been rewarding. To Shamid Austin, you are an inspiration to all young men. To my cousin, Jovan Johnson, you are my hero. To Beverly Johnson, without whom I would not have met Joy and realized my dream. To Teresa Hernandez, when other colleges told me not to even apply, you gave me hope and helped me to get into college. Thank you for your support. To Rochelle Tominlson and Quanza Kent, thank you for reading my manuscript and offering your honest opinions. To Bible Way Christian Center in San Jose, California, Alondra Church of Christ, and the City of Refuge family, thank you for being places of spiritual growth and maturity. To Joylynn Jossel, thank you for giving me a chance to live my dream and for giving great tips on writing.

Finally, thank you—the reader. Out of all the books in the bookstores and libraries, you chose my book, and I am thankful for your support. I pray that this story will minister to you and at the very least, entertain you. God bless you all!

ROAD TO GETHSEMANE

CHAPTER ONE

"Father, forgive me for my unbelief." Timothy, the youth pastor at Gethsemane Church, uttered these words in an empty sanctuary. After two hours of non-stop prayer, Timothy's goatee clashed against the maroon carpet and started to itch. He had laid face first on the floor until his knees felt tender.

"Lord, I've never questioned your will, but I don't know if I can do what you're asking of me. I need you to guide me because I don't want to bring shame to the cross."

The devil saw opportunity in the placid moments of Timothy's meditation. *You're too weak for this. You will fail, and everyone will turn on you.*

An image of Constance popped into his head. At first, Timothy dismissed the thought as a distraction from Satan, but the image soon returned and was accompanied by a sense of trepidation. Though perplexed, Timothy began to pray for Constance. After several minutes, the need to pray for Constance had not ceased. Timothy got off the floor, exited the gloomy sanctuary, and headed toward the church secretary's office.

"I need Constance's number," Timothy said.

Emerald, his wife of five years, pulled away from her desk and grabbed a thick blue binder. The sanctuary's scent of pine oil was replaced with the scent of jasmine in Emerald's office.

"Is this in regards to the gospel concert idea you have?" Emerald asked.

"No, she's just weighing heavily in my spirit." Timothy scratched his goatee.

Emerald had done something different with her hair. She had experimented with a color that Timothy could best describe as a carrot orange. He thought the color blended well with her chestnut skin and brown eyes.

"You did something different with your hair," he remarked.

"I dyed it a week ago; thanks for noticing." Emerald wrote down Constance's phone number on a Post-it note. "You shot out of that meeting earlier with a quickness. I was going to ask how it went."

He made it a point not to keep anything from his wife, but what had transpired in Ananias's office a few hours ago had left Timothy confused.

"We'll talk about it later. It's going to be a long week; I can feel it," Timothy said.

"How was school?" Emerald knew to change the subject.

"Trying to teach seventh graders Language Arts on a Monday is like talking to a brick wall. There is, of course, Vernon who's extremely active in class, and as a teacher, that's always a plus."

Timothy began to dial Constance's number on his cell phone. Upon the sound of the ring tone, he exited Emerald's office.

On the fourth ring, Constance's voicemail came on. "Hello, you've reached Constance Anderson. I am unable to get to the phone right now, but please leave your name and a brief message, and I will get back to you as soon as possible. Thank you and God bless!"

"Hello, Constance. This is Pastor Wells. You're probably at work, but give me a call as soon as possible. You were weighing heavy on my heart, and I decided to give you a call to see if everything is all right. Call me back as soon as possible."

Timothy hung up the phone and went outside for a breath of fresh air. Gray clouds smothered the sky. The wind grazed his skin and left chill bumps as it easily blew away the red and yellow leaves.

Ananias Jones, the senior pastor at Gethsemane, came outside and stood next to Timothy. He looked like he was made out of stone, and he dwarfed the average-height Timothy.

"Well, it looks like it's going to rain," Ananias said.

"Looks like it," Timothy agreed.

"Listen, son, I know that I put a lot on your mind, but the good Lord put this on my heart, and I have to be obedient."

"I don't know if I could do what you and God are asking of me." Timothy turned toward Ananias.

"Timothy, I wouldn't ask you to do something that you wouldn't need the Lord's help to do."

"You know this will cause uproar, and a lot of people will be upset."

"This ain't a popularity contest." Ananias turned to Timothy.

"People will leave." Timothy's eyes held the weight of the world.

"The people who will leave, you don't need." Ananias put his hand on Timothy's shoulder. "My job has always been to get people to follow God, not follow me. My purpose has been to build my Father's house, and that's it."

CHAPTER TWO

The tall, pale-skinned doctor held a blood-smeared, knife-edged plastic tube in his hand. It was an image cemented into Constance's brain. Constance's eyes turned bloodshot red as her mahogany skin glistened from the sweat and tears. The pain could not be compared to anything Constance had ever experienced.

"Ms. Anderson, you must hold still. This is a very dangerous procedure. You can get an infection or worse," the doctor said through his mask.

Constance's lanky body squirmed on the gurney as she fought off the Asian nurse. "It hurts."

Only two minutes into the five-minute procedure, Constance searched her diminutive will to find enough nerve and strength to make it through the next three minutes.

"Finish!" Constance demanded as she swallowed her saliva.

"Okay, I'm going to need you to be very still," the doctor said.

"Okay!" She just wanted to get the ordeal over with.

The doctor reinserted the tube and Constance gripped

the railing until a sharp pain went through her hands. One second later, everything on the inside of her stomach was being torn apart and sucked out by a vacuum-like machine.

"All done," the doctor declared before he removed his blood-covered latex gloves and disposed of them in a nearby trashcan. He washed his hands in the sink next to the trashcan, while the nurse disposed of the contents from the aspirator.

The soreness from her cervix made it difficult for Constance to move. She touched her stomach, and tears fell from her eyes, but a smile soon emerged. She let out a sigh of relief. She had survived the procedure, and now she could move on with her life.

For the next two days, Constance drifted in and out of sleep. Her mind shifted from the procedure to the protesters who had stood outside of the clinic with posters of crushed baby skulls and destroyed fetuses.

Murderer! God is going to get you! Those words resounded in her ears.

On the third day, Constance got out of bed. She cried so much that her eyes and nose felt sore. She stumbled over empty yogurt cartons and water bottles as she made her way to the bathroom.

She was still a little numb when she used the restroom. Constance returned to her bed, but then decided that after two complete days without contact with anyone, she needed to check her phone messages.

Her legs felt like sandbags as she pushed herself off of her queen-sized bed and grabbed the black cordless phone from the charger.

"First voice message," the automated system said.

"Girl, you won't believe what's going down at the job. Folks are tripping around here. Terry walked out over some drama. I think I might need to take a few days off myself. But

I hope you feel better. I know you've been getting caught up on *General Hospital.* You're going to have to fill me in later. Love you. Bye!"

Tonya's message sparked a giggle from Constance before she deleted it.

"Next message," the automated system said.

"Please call American Express at 1-800-322-6262," was the next message. Constance deleted that one too.

"Next message," the automated system repeated once again.

"Hello, Constance, this is Pastor Wells. You're probably at work, but give me a call as soon as possible. You were weighing heavy on my heart, and I decided to give you a call to see if everything is all right. Call me back as soon as possible."

"What are you doing calling me?" Constance said underneath her breath before going to the next message.

"What's up, Constance? It's your boy, Kevin. I've been trying to get in contact with you all week. We need you in the studio. We got an album to finish. Hit me up. One!"

Constance exited her voicemail system and speed-dialed Kevin's cell phone number.

"Hello," Kevin answered.

"Hey," Constance said.

"What's good, baby girl?"

"Sick." Constance let out a moan to back up her claim.

"Is that right? What? You need me to come over there? Make you some chicken noodle soup. Some Progresso?"

Constance laughed. "You're so stupid!"

"On the real though, baby girl, we need you in the studio to finish this album. The label company is getting real antsy."

"I know, I know, and I'm sorry, but I just haven't been feeling well."

"Don't trip. You ain't got to apologize to me, but we need to get you in here ASAP."

"I know, but I'm not feeling well. I don't want to get in the studio and waste your time."

"I just need you to get down here, that's all. I got this tight track that I want you to bless. You know how we do. You get down here and the Spirit gets to moving, and before you know it, we may have two or three songs done by the end of the night. But I need you to get down here."

Constance could not remember the last time she brushed either her teeth or her hair, or when she had even taken a bath. She did not desire to sing for the Lord that night. "When do you want me to come in?"

"Tonight."

"Tonight? Oh, you tripping, I'm not coming out tonight."

"Baby girl, you've been a ghost lately. Canceling sessions, not returning phone calls; you got me boxed in."

Constance looked at the calendar on the wall, which gave daily scriptures. The scripture for Wednesday, October 13th was Psalms 91:1. She marked her studio dates and realized that the last time she was in the studio was on October 4th .

"I didn't plan on leaving the house today."

"I don't know what to tell you, but we need to get this done."

"Okay, okay!" Constance rubbed her forehead.

"Cool, I'll see you at seven PM."

Constance's gold watch read 3:46 PM. There was no way she could be ready in a couple of hours, and she knew Kevin would probably have her in the studio all night working on the song.

Mentally, it was too soon for Constance to go back to work on her sophomore album, but she had been unreliable lately in regards to her studio appearances, and there was only so much the label would put up with. The whole purpose of the abortion was to save her career. If the label did not release her album, then she would have gone through the whole ordeal for nothing.

Constance could not listen to gospel music in the car. In silence, her mind revisited the waiting room at the clinic.

Despite her best efforts, Constance failed to convince herself that she was only disposing of tissue, so she focused on her purpose and how she could go on with her career without the burden of an unwanted pregnancy.

"I'm thinking about going with this style for my birthday party." The young girl pointed at a hairstyle in the magazine she had been flipping through.

"That will look real nice on you." Constance leaned over to look at the picture.

"I can't wait to turn sixteen," the young girl said.

"My sweet sixteen was a blur," Constance replied.

Constance filled out the questionnaire. Her stomach did somersaults as she waited.

"Is this your first time?" the young girl asked.

"Yeah. What about you?"

"Second."

Constance could not believe that this fifteen-year-old girl was going through her second procedure with ease, while she could barely sit straight. Moments later, she found herself in a hospital gown in a cold, off-white room.

Her mind would only allow her to reflect up until that point. The events that followed were too horrific for Constance to recount. She used the right sleeve of her gray wool jacket to wipe away her tears.

She sped through the traffic light that turned red just as she crossed the intersection. She looked at her speedometer which fluctuated between 60 and 65 miles per hour.

The speed sign read: SPEED LIMIT 45 MPH." Constance released her foot off the accelerator.

Get it together. You don't need a ticket.

* * *

Constance sat in the parking lot of Platinum Studios. Her cell phone rang, but she did not answer it. She checked the caller ID and it showed a missed call from James, her boyfriend of one year.

"I don't have time to deal with this." Constance tossed the phone back into her purse.

The cell phone made a hard clicking sound, and Constance checked her purse to make sure she had not broken anything. She discovered that the cell phone had hit a copy of her first CD, *To God Be the Glory*. The cover had a picture of her with no makeup or lipstick, just her natural mahogany skin, hazel eyes, and full lips. On the cover she gave a smile that conveyed an unspeakable joy.

But when Constance stared at the mirror on her sun visor, she realized that she was miles away from the girl she was on the CD cover. She went into her purse and pulled out mascara. She untwisted the cap and removed the brush.

Constance then began to brush her eyelashes upward. She dipped her brush back into the container and repeated the process, but only on her right eye. She tightened the cap and tossed the mascara back in the makeup bag.

She then pulled out red lipstick from her purse. She pressed her lips together in a kissing motion and made a full circle around her lips. She rotated the lipstick from right to left on her bottom lip and covered untouched areas. Constance placed the lipstick back in her purse and pulled out a turquoise comb.

After straightening out the tangled parts of her shoulder-length black hair, Constance placed the comb back in her purse and closed it. She checked back in the mirror and flashed a smile before she closed the sun visor.

Constance entered into a modest-sized recording studio where Kevin sat on the switchboard mixing a song. James sat next to Kevin in a black leather chair, bobbing his head to the beat. Constance tried to back out upon seeing James, but Kevin saw her.

"About time you showed up," Kevin said.

James turned around with his sable skin and smiled at Constance. She had not expected to see him, and if she had known that he was at the studio with Kevin, she would have cancelled.

"When did you get back?" Constance asked James, not replying to Kevin's comment.

"I landed this morning, I've been calling you, but you act like you don't know how to answer your phone," James replied.

"I've been busy." Constance was being short.

"Definitely not in the studio," Kevin interrupted.

"Hush." Constance cut her eyes at Kevin.

James stood up and walked over to Constance. "Let's go outside for a minute."

She folded her arms and turned toward the door. James opened the door for her, and they both exited.

"So? what's up, ma?" James asked.

"You tell me. You go on tour and forget you got a woman at home."

"You already know how crazy it is when you're on tour. What you want me to do? Check in every thirty minutes to put your mind at ease?"

"I don't need you to do nothing, because you're obviously going to do what you want to do anyway. Every time I look up, you're on tour, and you expect us to maintain a stable relationship that way?"

"Where's all this coming from? If you miss Big Daddy then say so, but don't come at me with this LoJack stuff, because you know I ain't going for it. Now, why don't you stop fronting like you really mad at me?" James walked up to Constance with a smile and tried to kiss her.

Constance moved out of the way. "Please. You won't be

getting this any time soon." Constance put her hand up to block James from kissing her.

"Here you go. Our church must've had one of those revivals or something, because you want to act like you're all holy now." James leaned in again and started to kiss Constance on the neck.

Constance's sensual weakness was her neck, and James knew that, but what he did not know was that his kisses had an adverse effect on Constance. "Listen, I got work to do." Constance pulled away.

"Okay then, but you and I have some things to discuss. Call me later."

"Okay. Yeah . . . whatever." Constance's hand flared in the air.

James pulled her chin toward him with his hand, and despite the resistance, he stole a small kiss on the lips. He then walked away toward the exit doors of the studio and chuckled to himself. Constance let out a sigh and went back into the studio.

"You're not sick!" Kevin said as Constance reentered the studio.

"I am sick."

"You don't sound sick."

"I'm not as sick as I was on Monday, but I'm still sick. That's why I didn't want to go out in the cold and come here. And how come you didn't tell me James was here?"

"I figured it would be a surprise."

"Negro, that wasn't a surprise."

"You guys have a falling out?"

"We never really have a falling out, which is part of the problem. He doesn't take anything serious, and he thinks I'm tripping because I do." Constance rolled her eyes.

"I was shocked to find out that his tour was over. You know him—he stays gone," Kevin said.

Therein lay another problem with Constance and James's

relationship. He was always on tour and she was always in the studio. This was no kind of environment to raise a child in. That fact allowed her to feel a little bit more comfortable with the decision she had made earlier that week.

"Hello." Kevin snapped his fingers to get Constance's attention. Once he had it, he continued. "I thought he was supposed to be touring with Kirk Franklin, but he told me he just finished touring with Darnell," Kevin said.

"Darnell offered him more money; he got one foot in the church and one foot in the world."

"There's too many of us that are like that. There are not too many genuine gospel artists out there," Kevin said.

"Every time I turn around I'm hearing about so-and-so doing a song with a secular artist. James feels like if they can get money with a secular artist, why can't he?" Constance shrugged.

"But that ain't going to be you, though. You're a genuine gospel artist." Kevin then added, "Yeah, that's what I like about you; you never try to be something that you're not."

"Thank you," Constance said with a half-smile.

"Anyways, let me let you listen to this track."

Kevin pressed a button on the switchboard and a song began to play. The melody was very smooth, a jazzy beat with an emphasis on the sound of the keyboard.

Constance reclined in the black leather chair next to Kevin with her arm on the armrest and her right hand underneath her chin. They nodded their heads to the beat.

"That's tight . . . that's real smooth," Constance complimented.

"As they say in New York, that's that jump-off right here. You would do your thing on this beat. You got that anointing," Kevin threw a compliment right back.

"What were you thinking about as far as angles?" Constance asked.

"I was thinking of us doing it like a love song, but we can flip it and instead of you talking about a man, you're talking about God."

"Okay, okay." Constance nodded

"Could you pen this one?" Kevin asked.

"I don't know. I think you're in a better frame of mind," Constance said.

"I can't write like you."

"I'm not feeling it, though," Constance said.

"Constance, I need you to tap into your anointing and pull out another song. We are seriously working against the clock." Kevin rubbed his forehead back and forth several times.

"I know, I know. But I just can't do it tonight."

"You can do all things—"

"Through Christ Jesus that strengthens me. I know, but I'm not feeling well." Constance started to rub her head.

Kevin turned off the song and put his head down. "Constance, your last album did cool, but it didn't really get any pub, and it wasn't really distributed outside the Bay market. But it still managed to move enough units for the label to decide to put real support behind this album." Kevin lifted up his head. "They want to get you on the radio and maybe even a tour, but it all comes down to what we do here. If we put in enough time to produce a quality product, then that's what we'll get. I need you here, right now."

Kevin's words sailed through Constance's eardrums, but her mind raced through the image of the doctor with a blood-smeared tube and the nurse, who tried violently to restrain Constance. Constance pulled a small package of Kleenex out of her purse. She wiped the tears from her eyes and began to play with the tissue.

"You're not going to get quality work out of me tonight. I'm sorry, but I'm not in that place," she told Kevin.

"You need to find it quick." Kevin turned toward the switchboard.

"I will. It's just that this week is not a good week. I got a lot of things going on. Let's try to hook up next week."

Kevin rubbed his head. "All right, that's cool."

Constance walked over behind Kevin and gave him a hug. She tried to give him a kiss, but Kevin fought it away.

"Come on, don't be that way. You know I love you like a stepbrother," she said.

"No, you don't. You're over here playing. You know I got kids to feed and baby mommas to pay."

"I'm sorry," Constance said.

"Anyways, how's church?" Kevin asked.

"It's cool. You remember that youth pastor I told you about? Timothy?" Constance asked.

"Yeah, young dude," Kevin said.

"He left me an urgent message, talking about I was on his heart."

"Oh no, not another Reverend Pimp Daddy." Kevin chuckled.

"No, not that. But still, I'm not sure about dude. I don't know if he's trying to get over or not. He's been doing a lot lately. I don't know, I guess I'm a skeptic when it comes to ministers."

"Not with the mighty Pastor Ananias Jones," Kevin said.

"Pastor Jones is a dying breed. They don't anoint pastors like him anymore. He's a genuine person," Constance said.

"Maybe this young pastor is genuine."

"I don't know, though. I mean, I don't have a particular incident, but there is just something about him that I find sneaky," Constance said.

"I think you're over-analyzing. Pastor Jones is getting up there in age; dude may be your next pastor," Kevin reasoned.

"Please, Pastor Childs is the associate pastor. Ananias wouldn't pick Timothy over the associate pastor," Constance said.

"You never know. He has to do what the Spirit is leading him to do." Kevin shrugged. "And remember, God's way may not necessarily be man's way."

CHAPTER THREE

Only one police car had passed by in the last ten minutes, which was rare even on this side of town. The sun started to recede behind the clouds as Darius sat in his pearl white Escalade that was parked between two compact cars. With the stereo turned down so low that the lyrics of the song could not be understood, Darius massaged the trigger of his glock.

From the rearview mirror, he examined his freshly trimmed, wavy black hair and goatee. His skin matched the color of his glock, and his ensemble consisted of a polo shirt and khaki pants.

A tall, lanky individual who wore a black T-shirt down to his knees with a black baseball cap caught Darius's attention. He turned off the stereo and exited his SUV; cocked his gun and released a bullet into the chamber. The young man heard the clicking sound of Darius's gun. Before he could react, Darius smacked him on the right side of his face with the butt of the gun. The young man's legs buckled from the impact, and he collapsed onto the ground.

Darius walked around to the left side of the young man

and kicked him in the shoulders so that he lay flat on his back. His eyes bulged at the sight of Darius.

The edge of Darius's gun made the young man's face virtually disappear.

"Fourteenth and Williams Street. Do you know that area?" Darius asked with a blank stare.

The young man's eyes rotated from right to left, and then they stopped.

"No, I don't," the young man said.

"You sure?" Darius asked.

"Yeah!" the young man insisted.

"Cool, then that means that I shouldn't ever see you over there, not even by accident. Because word is bond, yo—if I catch you violating the block again, I won't come back to talk." Darius's eyes were void of emotion.

Darius had never murdered anyone, but the way he held his gun with confidence and certainty, he gave off the prowess equivalent to a stone cold killer. He looked up and started to back away. He looked both ways as he crossed the street. He stopped in the middle of the street to let a green car pass before he got back into his Escalade and drove off.

After he pulled away, the young man stood up and yelled obscenities. Darius turned his stereo up too loud for him to make out what the young man had yelled.

Timothy walked the streets of San Jose. He stepped over broken glass and passed by palm trees with graffiti written on them. Timothy was convinced that if Jesus were on earth today, then he would be walking the streets in the midst of condemned apartment buildings, broken pavement, and liquor stores, preaching the Gospel.

On Fourteenth and Williams Street, the drug dealers and their clientele were Timothy's last stops on an otherwise fruitless evening.

Timothy stood outside his black Ford and considered the

fact that it would be easier to put a needle through a cement block than to reach these young drug dealers.

Chris had joined the church three weeks ago and had immediately approached Timothy with a desire to go out and witness. After some reservation, Timothy acknowledged Chris as the second member of the evangelism team. Though short in stature, Chris had managed to maintain his football player's physique. Timothy handed him a handful of tracts, information cards that offered the prayer of salvation and information regarding the church. It also had a scripture, John 3:16.

"It's just us?" Chris asked.

"I called Elder Childs, but he did not return my message," Timothy informed him.

Though he always felt a little discomfort when he went out, Timothy never sensed that he was in danger because he grew up around neighborhoods similar to those in San Jose. His discomfort came from tension of preaching the Gospel to people who lacked hope and faith.

"You'll be fine. Just remember we don't have to convince them. You just have to put the Word out, plant the seed," Timothy said.

When the drug dealers caught a glimpse of Timothy and Chris, their laughter ceased, and they stood up, waiting for the two strangers to approach. Their breath reeked of alcohol and marijuana.

Timothy had mentally prepared an introduction, but it disappeared upon his arrival at the street corner. He did not know what to say. A boy who stood head and shoulders above his two companions appeared to be the leader of the three. He wore a black beanie and a black peacock coat. The boy next to him looked about the same age, but he was slumped over with his hands in his pocket. Timothy figured he was self-conscious about his obesity. The shortest of them all was undoubtedly the youngest.

"God has not given us the spirit of fear nor timidity, but of love, power, and a sound mind," Timothy reminded himself underneath his breath.

"What up?" The tall boy gave Timothy a head nod.

"What's going on? My name is Timothy, and this is Brother Chris." He pointed. "And we just wanted to invite you to our church."

"Rich," the tallest boy introduced himself. "What church do you guys go to?" Rich asked.

"Gethsemane Community Church," Chris replied.

"I've already got a church home . . . over there off of . . . off of . . ." The heavyset boy snapped his fingers.

"Kalil, you stupid. You ain't been to church since Easter," Rich said.

"You got hoes there?" Kalil asked Timothy.

"Listen, brothers, we just stopped by to tell you that God loves you and He has a plan for your life," Timothy said.

"He's got a plan for me?" the youngest asked.

"He has a plan for all of us," Timothy replied.

"I don't know, man; it looks like I'm doing a lot better than you. You rolled up here in a Ford. I probably got enough money in my pocket to buy that off you," Rich said to Timothy as he pulled out a cigarette. "Marshall here too." He nodded to the youngest of the three boys.

"But do you have peace?" Timothy asked.

Rich looked away and took a puff of his cigarette. Timothy sensed that his last statement had penetrated his heart.

"What's the sense of getting money if you're constantly looking over your shoulders, worrying about the cops, your enemies, and fiends?" Timothy asked. "Come on, man, I know the game. I've had family caught up in the dope game and they'll tell you from behind bars that it's not worth it. When God gives you wealth, He adds no sorrow."

"Man, miss me with all that," Marshall hissed. "People like you feed my mom that same line, and every week she pours her money into the preacher's pocket. He rolls in a Caddy while she barely makes ends meet. That's until I got on the grind. Y'all be over there robbing folks," Marshall replied.

"And how many families are you robbing?" Timothy asked.

"I'm feeding my family," Marshall said.

"God doesn't want you to destroy other families in order to take care of yours. I know how hard it is, and I know that you may have come across some shady folks in the past who called themselves Christians, but you can't let that stop you from having a personal relationship with Jesus Christ," Timothy said.

"Man, I probably sold crack to some of your members," Marshall said before he let out a laugh.

"You may be right, but you're still in need of a savior." Timothy handed each guy an invitation card to Gethsemane Community Church.

"Look, all we want is for you guys to visit our church. See for yourself what God has for you," Chris said.

"Whatever, fam," Marshall said.

"God bless you!" Chris said.

"All right, y'all," Rich replied.

Timothy turned around and he felt somewhat proud of his accomplishment.

"That was intense." Chris let out a sigh of relief.

"But that was the ministry that Jesus walked and lived," Timothy reminded him.

Darius parked his truck a block away from where Marshall and his boys hung out. He saw two men get into a black Ford and drive off. Darius reclined in his seat and reflected on home.

He did not miss Jersey, but he did miss home. In a strange way, he missed the warmth that came from eight bodies packed in a three-bedroom shack. He knew his family did not approve of how he earned his money, but they could not resist the fact that food remained on the table and the lights were on.

Darius had the block sewn up before a fatal incident caused him to flee to California two years ago in search of a new life, but California offered the same hustle, just a different time zone. On most days, he managed to convince himself that he had left Jersey to protect his family, but in the back of his mind, Darius felt like a coward.

He opened his eyes and took a sip from his energy drink. He smacked his lips from the bitter aftertaste, exited his truck, and felt the cool evening air brush across his face. He threw the empty can on the ground and put on his black beanie as he walked up to Rich and his boys. When Rich saw Darius, he got the attention of the other two. They straightened up and looked serious. Darius loved respect as much as he loved money; on some days, he preferred respect.

"What up, D?" Rich asked.

"What's good with you?" Darius said.

They balled their hands into a fist and pounded them against each other. Rich handed Darius the church flyer.

"You know you need Jesus!" Rich patted Darius on the shoulder and giggled.

Darius laughed as he put the flyer in his back pocket. "I'm gonna hold onto this because breezies be at the church house on Sunday, repenting for shaking it up at the club the night before," Darius said.

Darius surveyed the territory. A homeless man dug into a Dumpster, a young boy rode his bike down the middle of the street, and a grandmother stood outside the apartment complex in rollers and her nightgown. He assumed she was awaiting her grandson's return home.

"Are y'all getting it or what?" Darius asked.

"It's slow tonight; not too many customers, plus it's cold," Rich said, rubbing his hands together and blowing his hot breath into them.

"This ain't cold. I'll take you back to Jersey and show you cold." Darius realized that Marshall, Rich's younger brother, was on the block as well.

"Yo, what your brother doing here?" Darius asked Rich.

"I'm trying to get caked out like you guys," Marshall said.

"Man, you don't need to be out here with us. You need to be at a shorty's house or something."

"Relax, D. I said it's cool." Rich walked toward Darius

"Did I say it's cool? This my block, and if I don't want your brother hustling, then guess what? He won't be hustling."

"Come on, Darius. I won't cause any trouble, and I'll listen to everything you say," Marshall begged.

"You need to stay sharp and hungry to seriously get your money."

"I got you," Marshall said.

"All right then, we'll test you out and see if you can handle it," Darius said.

"Did you handle that?" Rich asked.

Darius started to laugh hysterically. "Word is bond, yo. Son was shook. His eyes looked like a cartoon, yo! Son won't deal on this side of town ever again," Darius boasted.

A man in a flannel shirt with dirty jeans walked up to Darius. He nervously scratched his vein.

"What's good with you, Sam?" Darius asked upon recognizing the man.

"I just need two," Sam said.

"What you got?" Darius went into his pocket.

"Fifteen."

"Sam, you know you need a minimum twenty." Darius took his hands out of his pocket.

"Russ lets me pay fifteen," Sam said.

"If you ain't got twenty, you ain't getting high tonight." Darius stepped away from Sam and leaned against a palm tree that was next to him.

Sam started to scratch his arm and tremble. "Come on, baby—hook your boy up."

"Shake, man!" Darius waved his hand at Sam.

"Come on, just this one time." Sam was desperate.

"Get out of here!" Darius flinched toward Sam, and Sam took off the other way. Darius looked directly at Rich. "You better holla at ya mans. It's okay to take the short every now and again, but he got cats thinking that we're a high-for-less."

"I'll talk to him," Rich assured Darius.

A silver car appeared and a guy in a two-piece suit, minus the tie, got out and walked across the street. Darius met him on the edge of the sidewalk.

"What's going on, Walter?" Darius asked.

"Nothing. I need four," Walter said.

Darius reached into his pocket and pulled out a plastic bottle with a black cap. The bottle had four little white rocks with a little bit of a powdery substance on the bottom. Darius exchanged the bottle for two twenty-dollar bills.

"Thank you." Walter turned around and headed back to his car and drove off.

"He still works at the bank," Darius said.

"I wonder if he be robbing his job." Rich watched him drive away.

"It don't matter, as long as he pays," Darius said.

"Your Nets got whooped tonight by San Antonio." Kalil changed the subject.

"We still going to make the playoffs, unlike your whack Warriors that ain't been to the playoffs since C. Web was on their team," Darius said.

"That's all right, though. We're going to make trades in the off-season and get a good draft pick. Watch!" Kalil said.

"Yeah, that's what you and the Clippers say every year." Darius laughed

A black Monte Carlo with tinted windows and loud music

pulled up within three blocks of Darius and his crew. The car moved slowly and suspiciously, and Darius became uneasy at the sight.

The window rolled down and the car started to speed toward them.

"Move!" Darius warned his comrades. Without hesitation, Darius dashed toward the end of the block. He did not look back. His mind was already around the corner; he just needed for his legs to catch up. He heard screams and the obscenities of his crew. The muscles in his legs inflamed from exhaustion. Shots fired, loud and sporadic, and the engine roared as the car got closer and closer. Darius turned the corner and nearly tripped over his feet as his hand touched the concrete and he took off again in a sprinter's position.

Darius cut into an alley of an apartment complex and hid behind a big green Dumpster. A violent heartbeat allowed him only short breaths. The car shot past Darius as he pulled out his glock. He started to jog toward the end of the alley, hunched over. Police would be on the scene at any moment. Darius had to get back to his truck.

When he arrived at the end of the alley, the car had slowed down near the end of the block. Darius ran out into the street and started to shoot at the car. His first shot took out the back window, and the car sped away as the person in the passenger seat shot back at Darius. He ran back toward the alley. The gunshots awoke the whole neighborhood. The frantic neighbors and loud barking dogs did not faze Darius as he dashed through the apartments.

His only concern was to get back to his truck before the Monte Carlo came back or the police showed up. He climbed over the metal gate with ease and sprinted to the other side of the apartment complex. He unloaded the drugs and his gun in a nearby sewer drain. He kept his spare gun in the truck. His Escalade remained parked at end of the block. Not a soul was in sight.

He sprinted toward his truck and turned off his alarm. He got into his truck, and before he knew it, two shots pierced through his window and hit him in the chest. The impact felt like a sledgehammer. Darius slumped to the left, and another bullet whisked by his ear and pierced through his car's headrest.

The car stopped, another car door slammed, and Darius's car door opened. He could not make out any distinct facial features, but he did see that the person wore a black cap. Startled by the sight of the gun barrel, Darius tried to breathe one last healthy breath. "Lord, please forgive me."

The trigger snapped, but no bullet discharged. The shooter pulled the trigger again and again. No bullet. Sirens started to close in, and the shooter fled the scene. The sirens got louder and louder until the tires of the ambulance screeched as it came to a halt. Darius slipped out of consciousness.

CHAPTER FOUR

It started with an email pop-up that led to a porn site. Dennis scrolled through pictures of stark-naked women. Extremely aroused, the pictures burned into his memory. When condemnation set in, Dennis would delete the link and erase the history of the link from his computer. He spent the next couple of hours torn between numbers from last year's fiscal profits for his construction company and naked women.

For eleven years, he had served faithfully as associate pastor at Gethsemane.

"Lord, please forgive me for lusting after other women."

His secretary, Cecilia, a Puerto Rican with a Coke-bottle figure and a scent of a rose, entered his office. She wore a dress that accentuated her breasts. Dennis bit his fat bottom lip to conceal his desire for her.

"Papi, here's the numbers from last quarter."

"Thank you. Just leave them on the desk."

After she placed a handful of files on his desk, he turned to the left and continued to work on his computer. In his periphery, Cecilia stood at attention.

"Is there anything you need?" Cecilia asked.

Dennis glanced up and stood. He threw her on top of his desk and ripped open her blouse before he snapped back to reality.

"No, thank you. I'm good. I just got to get this done."

Cecilia walked over to Dennis and his body tightened up as her firm, soft hands caressed his shoulders. His middle-weight boxer's physique balanced out his receding hairline, and he knew that Cecilia enjoyed massaging his shoulders. She leaned so that her lips were an inch away from his ear and whispered, "Don't worry; everything will work out with the audit."

Goosebumps sprang up on Dennis's neck. "I hope so. We're just starting to get going, and the last thing I need is the IRS slowing us up."

Cecilia patted Dennis on the shoulders.

"I'll stay here all night if I have to," Cecilia declared.

"Thanks. I appreciate it." Dennis turned toward his computer and started to type.

"How's your little ones?"

Upon Cecilia's question. Dennis glanced at the picture of his two beautiful children: eight-year-old Elijah in a baseball uniform, and Jasmine, who was four about to turn twenty-nine.

"They're great. Doing well in school."

"That's good. I have a meeting with my son Miguel's teacher tonight," Cecilia said.

Cecilia brushed her hand against his forearm and Dennis was aroused. At that moment, he wanted to throw principle out the door long enough to indulge in a moment of passion without any regret.

"I'll come back later for that data report," Cecilia said, patting her boss on the shoulder and walking away.

"Sounds good," Dennis replied.

Dennis stared at her butt until he noticed that Cecilia

looked back at the reflection in the mirror on his office door. Dennis put his head down and pretended to be busy at work. Though she had left his office, her scent remained.

Dennis often made up reasons why she needed to visit his office, and then stumbled over explanations of what he needed for her to complete. He knew God's grace sustained fidelity in his marriage. He prayed it did, anyway.

CHAPTER FIVE

Thursday night, Vernon found himself on first and goal, with the Dallas Cowboys about to score. His thumb ached from pressing the buttons of the controller so hard, but the idea that he could beat his uncle Alex in Madden NFL gave him all the motivation he needed.

"The pressure is on. You better not try that play on T.O.," his uncle said.

"Don't worry about what I'm doing; just get ready to hand me my five dollars."

Vernon's uncle turned up the volume on his surround sound, and the simulated stadium crowd made a thunderous noise as Vernon moved his men to the line of scrimmage. Vernon pressed the button to hike the ball and, sure enough, had the quarterback throw it to T.O., who scored the touchdown. Vernon leapt to his feet in celebration, and Alex pounded the floor.

"You got lucky," his uncle said.

"Don't hate, Uncle. I beat you straight up," Vernon bragged. When Vernon was not doing his school work from Mr. Wells, he enjoyed playing video games.

"That's just because we're playing on All-Pro. If we would've been playing on All-Madden mode, I would've blown you out."

"Whatever, Uncle." Vernon jumped up and down in victory.

"Hey, calm down. Your sister is in the next room asleep."

The clock read 11:53 PM. Vernon's mother would have never let him stay up this late on a Monday night, but thanks to her new boyfriend, Greg, who loved to see her all the time, Vernon and his younger sister, Autumn, would spend the majority of the time at their uncle's house. Vernon had access to all the latest video games and toys because his uncle was a kid at heart.

Uncle Alex picked up a pizza box that still had a few pepperoni slices left in it. "You want any more of this?" Vernon's uncle asked

"No thank you, Uncle."

"That's why you're so skinny now, because you don't eat," Alex said.

"I'm not skinny." Vernon pulled back the sleeve of one of his shirts and made a muscle.

"Boy, you're a toothpick if I ever seen one." Alex chuckled. "It's way past your bedtime. Get dressed, and go on to bed."

"Okay, Uncle."

Later that night, Vernon could not sleep, so he decided to get up and poke around. He crawled around the floor in the dark toward his uncle's partially cracked door, and a blue light prevailed from the room. Vernon crawled a little closer and knew that his uncle was watching the television. He stood outside his door and could hear moans, which caused him to giggle.

He surmised that his uncle must have had a dirty movie on. He lost control of his balance and banged up against the wall. The thud caused his uncle to jump up and open the door wide. He stood there with his shirt off, wearing only boxer shorts.

"Boy, what are you doing up?"

"Nothing, Uncle. I'm sorry."

"Get in here." Alex pointed to the inside of his room.

Vernon got up and went into the room, and his uncle closed the door behind him. Vernon looked at the TV and noticed that kids, not much older than he was, covered the screen. They were naked and blindfolded.

"You think that's cool to sneak up on your uncle, huh?" Alex scolded.

"No, Uncle, it's not. I'm sorry." Vernon held his head down.

Alex stared down at his nephew for a minute. Then he spoke. "Take off your shirt," Vernon's uncle demanded.

Vernon did not move. He tried to understand why his uncle owned a movie with naked little kids.

"Did you hear me? I said take it off!" Vernon's uncle grabbed his shirt and tried to take it off.

Vernon tried to lock his arms in, but Uncle Alex overpowered Vernon like a vicious beast. After he took off Vernon's shirt, he examined Vernon's thin body and let out a half-grin.

"Now take off your pants," he ordered.

"No, Uncle, please," Vernon said, tears starting to fall.

"Take those pants off now or I'm going to do it for you."

Vernon unfastened his belt and took off his pants. Down to just his underwear, his uncle locked the door and walked over his nephew.

CHAPTER SIX

Timothy felt knots in his lower back, caused by his oversized messenger bag. He missed the keyhole several times, until he finally held the doorknob with his left hand and used the key to unlock the door. Timothy could hear the Isley Brothers from the outside of his apartment.

When he opened the door, candles in the living room illuminated the entire apartment. On the dining room table were two candles and a blue dish filled with pasta.

"Hello, baby," Emerald greeted him.

A beautiful silhouette of his wife appeared at the other end of the room. She wore a maroon silk dress that accentuated her hips. Timothy froze at the sight of her. Her beauty signified two things: yes, there was a God, and He loved Timothy.

Emerald walked over and placed her hands on Timothy's chest. She slowly worked her way up to his shoulders and slipped his coat off of him. Timothy used his arms to pull off his jacket. Emerald took his jacket and tossed it on the couch. She took Timothy by the hand and led him to the kitchen table, where Timothy pulled out a chair for her.

"Thank you," Emerald said as she sat down.

"No problem."

Timothy sat directly across from Emerald as she used a serving spoon and dished pasta onto Timothy's plate. She served herself a small portion and set the plate down.

"Pray," Emerald said.

Timothy bowed his head. "Dear God, bless this food. May it be nourishing to our bodies. Take away anything that is harmful, and bless those who are less fortunate. In Jesus' name we pray. Amen."

"Amen," Emerald said. She then started a conversation with Timothy. "How was your day?"

"Trying to teach poetry to preteens is like trying to teach bees tricks."

"You know you love it."

"You're right, I do, and I can't say all of them are lost. There's this one kid, Vernon. Man, he's really into reading, and he's always participating in class. He gets teased by the other students, but it doesn't deter him."

"You're making a difference."

"It's nice to see I'm making a difference in something, because being over the evangelism ministry is in a lot of ways a thankless job."

"I almost forgot, Elder Childs called. He apologized for not being able to make it," Emerald said.

"What else is new?" Timothy ate as if he were in a hurry. He did not make eye contact with Emerald.

"Personally, I feel like I'm not getting any elbow room from Pastor. He's a great man of God, but the budget for the youth is a joke. And I think we should go witnessing on a different night, because mid-week witnessing is not working," Timothy said.

"Have you talked with Pastor about it?" Emerald took a bite of her food.

"I got a meeting with him tomorrow, and please believe it's not going to be about what we talked about the other day," Timothy said.

Emerald put her fork down and reached for Timothy's hand. For the first time, Timothy looked up, and Emerald smiled.

"What?" he asked.

"I love you so much. You're a great man of God and you're a great minister."

"I don't know, babe. After last night, I don't feel anything like a minister. You should've seen these kids on this one block—they were gone. They looked at me as if I was the fool. To them, God had left them a long time ago. How can you get through to them?"

Timothy finished his food. He walked over to Emerald and placed his hand on her warm cheek.

"You're going to go to bed, babe?" a disappointed Emerald asked.

"Yeah. Six AM will be here before I know it."

Timothy hated to disappoint his wife with yet another romantic night reduced to a routine conversation about ministry and purpose. But he lacked the strength to give her what she wanted.

The blood in Ananias's veins turned cold. The hospital gown left his back exposed enough for the cool central air to work its way through his spine. He wanted to sit up straight, but his lower back pain made hunching over more desirable.

The mint-green walls did very little to soothe him as Ananias fidgeted, so much that he tore a piece of the tissue that covered the gurney and twisted it into a little braid.

What's taking so long? he wondered.

The visit to the emergency room was sparked by a constant pain in his chest that felt like a hand had gripped his heart. Dr. Gaines, a medium-height and middle-aged doctor, seemed more concerned with his charts than eye contact with his patient.

"Okay, Mr. Jones, it looks like you have major clogged arteries. You haven't been eating healthy. And are you still a pastor at your church?" Dr. Gaines asked.

"I preach every service," Ananias said.

"How many hours of sleep are you getting?" Dr. Gaines asked as his eyes scanned the charts.

"About five, sometimes six," Ananias said.

Ananias's answer prompted a sour face from Dr. Gaines. "You need eight hours of sleep, especially a man your age. You have your heart working overtime. That's not good."

Because of the age difference, Ananias dismissed Dr. Gaines' advice as young and inexperienced. While Dr. Gaines looked to be in his mid-thirties, with invincible posture, Ananias had lived to see the hairs on his face grow back faster than the hairs on his head.

"I know you would like to stick around a little longer to play with your grandchildren," Dr. Gaines stated. "You do have grandchildren, don't you?"

"Yes, but I haven't seen my grandchildren in months, and I'm sure they're getting too old to play with."

Ananias kept a firm grip on reality. He knew that he would never be remembered as a great father. He chose to be known as a great preacher, and he chose Helen to be his wife and to understand that she married a first class preacher and a second class husband. Helen made their three children—Elijah, Samuel, and Beersheba—to understand that they could depend on her for all of the moral support and attendance at parent teacher conferences, and they could depend on their father for scripture and prayer. Helen had died nine years ago. Ananias could have drawn closer to his children, but instead he filled the void with countless speaking engagements.

"I can't stop preaching. I would go crazy if I did," Ananias said.

"All I know is either you slow down, or your body will make that decision for you. I'm going to give you a prescription and set up an appointment," Dr. Gaines scanned the charts again.

"That's fine!" Ananias said.

As Dr. Gaines left the room, Ananias methodically began to put on his clothes. After he put on his sports coat, he grabbed his Kangol hat and walked out of the room. He exchanged the quiet tranquility of the room he had been in for the chaos of several nurses as they rushed a body down the hall. A frantic woman was in hot pursuit behind them.

"God, please save my son!" the woman cried out.

Nurses rushed past him, and he caught a glimpse of a young man with his chest partially exposed from a blood-drenched shirt. Ananias sprinted after the woman until he was short of breath. He grabbed the railing for support as the checkered floor tiles became blurry.

"Strengthen me, Lord, so that I may do your will," he panted.

Ananias's air stopped mid-way up his chest. The woman's screams sent a jolt to his body. He cursed his ailment. The boy could be dead by now, and he may in fact die before he got a chance to accept Jesus as his Lord and Savior. Ananias used the railing to push himself up, and he briskly followed the mother's screams until he caught up with the boy.

The nurses restrained the frantic mother as the doctors worked feverishly to revive the young man. A tall doctor with a hunched back used the defibrillator and sent a jolt to the young man's body, but there was no response.

Ananias could not stomach the horrific scene. He took the responsibility of restraining the mother and allowed the nurses to assist. The mother did not notice the switch. Her eyes were transfixed on her son.

"Father, in the name of Jesus, we ask right now that you

spare the life of this young man," Ananias said above all the chaos.

"Yes, Lord; don't take away my Deshawn," the mother cried.

"Father, just like you brought back Lazarus, we know that you are more than capable of bringing back Deshawn. Hear our cry, oh Lord. Do not turn a deaf ear to our prayer. Revive Deshawn and we will give you all of the glory and praise. In Jesus' name, amen."

As Ananias's prayer concluded, the machine flat-lined. The mother dropped to her knees and let out moans that reverberated throughout the emergency room.

"No, Lord, please!" the mother said.

There were no more attempts to revive Deshawn. The doctors looked at one another quizzically. An air of failure filled the room. Ananias and the mother felt a grave disappointment.

Ananias did not notice the makeup on his collar from the mother's tears. With his hand over his mouth, he leaned back in his brown leather chair, puzzled by his unanswered prayer. From the hospital, he went straight to the church.

"He was only fifteen, Lord. I know you could've saved him and birthed a mighty ministry within him. There are too many of our young people you've allowed to be cut down due to senseless violence, and I don't question your will, but ask that you help your servant. What must I do to save this lost generation?"

Alone in his office with only God to hear him, Ananias took sips from the coffee Emerald had brought him twenty minutes ago as he stared at his large print Bible, opened to Second Chronicles 7:14-17.

"If my people, which are called by my name," Ananias read out loud, "shall humble themselves, and pray, and seek my face, and turn from their wicked ways; then will I hear from heaven, and will forgive their sin." Ananias closed the

Bible then asked himself, "Where have we gone wrong with the ministry? Did we drop the ball somewhere?"

His thoughts passed over the doctor's visit to the young boy who died that day to his sermon on Sunday. He even reflected upon the meeting with Timothy earlier in the week. God had placed it on Ananias's heart that Timothy would be his successor. Though there was a handful of men that Ananias thought were more qualified than Timothy to take over Gethsemane, Ananias was obedient and shared God's plan with Timothy.

Timothy, in turn, had gone into the sanctuary and prayed for more than two hours. That day, Ananias felt foolish for having told Timothy that he wanted him to take over. God had not given Ananias insight as to when He wanted him to hand the ministry over to Timothy, and with that uncertainty, he felt he may have scared Timothy off.

The morning's unfortunate events caused Ananias to put to rest any doubts he had about the direction in which God wanted the church to go. A pain arose in his chest. He grimaced, but quickly searched for a way to reduce his chest pain.

"Lord, relax your servant. By your stripes I am healed. Touch my body and relieve my pain."

The tension in his chest began to decrease. The pain receded. "Thank you, Jesus!" Ananias said before he heard a knock on his door. "Yes," Ananias said.

"Pastor, it's me, Timothy."

Ananias fixed his tie and wiped his forehead with a Kleenex. "Yes, come in."

Timothy entered Ananias's office with a wide smile. Ananias loved Timothy for his zeal and resiliency. His words and actions remained ministry-centered. Ananias hardly ever worried about Timothy.

"Good afternoon, sir," Ananias said.

"Good afternoon, Pastor."

"How may I help you?"

"I just wanted to talk to you about the evangelism ministry."

"Sure, sure! Can we discuss this over a game?" Ananias pointed to the corner of his office where a table with a chess game in progress stood.

"Definitely," Timothy gladly accepted.

Ananias took his seat up against the wall next to his bookshelf, while Timothy took his seat next to Ananias's plants. For several minutes, Ananias studied the chessboard and tried to recall where he had left off. The grin on Timothy's face indicated that he remembered.

"It's your move, Pastor," Timothy said.

Ananias moved his knight. "What's your question regarding? Witnessing?"

Timothy ignored Ananias's move and moved his rook. "Wednesday night witnessing is not working."

"Oh." Ananias was somewhat embarrassed by the news.

"I think we should move it to either Friday or Saturday night."

"How so?"

"Most of the young people go to the club on Saturday night. We can pass out tracts and witness to them before they even go into the club."

"Interesting."

The phone rang twice before Emerald spoke on the intercom.

"Pastor," Emerald spoke.

Ananias got up, but never took his eyes off the chessboard as he pressed the intercom button. "Yes?"

"Pastor Lewis from Freedom Fellowship is on the other line wanting to talk to you about their upcoming revival."

Ananias looked away from the chessboard and held up one finger to Timothy. "Put him through." He picked up the phone. "Hey, doc! How are you?"

"Living this life so I may live again," Pastor Lewis answered from the other end of the phone

"I hear you. What can I do for you?" Ananias asked.

"We're having a revival on February twelfth. I was wondering if you wouldn't mind bringing the Word?"

Ananias scanned over his calendar. "I don't have any prior engagements."

"Great! We'll put you on our bulletin, and I'll have guest services contact you."

"Okay then, sounds good." Ananias hung up the phone and immediately refocused his eyes back on the chessboard. "Now, where were we?"

"Wednesday night witnessing," Timothy reminded him.

Ananias snapped his fingers in remembrance.

"The problem with that is we already have service on Wednesday, so it is easier to get a couple of brothers to go with you downtown to pass out tracts. On Saturday, we would be asking them to take time away from their families."

"But no one is coming out! All anybody does is give excuses."

Ananias looked up and recognized the look on Timothy's face—eyes filled with frustration and voice on the brink of desperation. Ananias felt a sense of guilt for his lack of support for a faithful servant of God.

"I understand your frustration, but even still, you have to compel people to come out and share the gospel. I thought Elder Childs was working with you."

"So did I," Timothy said sharply.

Ananias further understood Timothy's frustration. People in the ministry who made a proclamation to build the ministry surrounded him, but when the time came to put words into action, they suddenly disappeared.

"He hasn't gone out?" Ananias asked.

"No. He won't even return my phone calls. He waits until

service on Sunday, and then he apologizes for not returning my call."

Ananias had to admit that he had noticed a decrease in Elder Childs' commitment level. A few years ago, Elder Childs would have been his successor without question, but when he started his construction company, members started to see him less.

"Timothy, there's something the good Lord put on my heart many years ago, and I am going to share it with you."

"Okay, Pastor." Timothy sat at attention.

"Do not be concerned with what everyone else is doing; God is concerned with what you're doing. And God is the one who promotes and corrects."

Ananias had said those exact words to Timothy before. But this time, he hoped that his words would make a way into Timothy's heart.

"I know, Pastor," Timothy said with his head down.

Timothy studied the next move, and Ananias studied Timothy. He loved Timothy like a son. He was a decent preacher, and maybe if Ananias gave him more microphone time, he might prove to be a great preacher. But in the five years since Timothy moved to San Jose from Los Angeles, integrity stood out as his best attribute.

"Have you ever thought about why you got into ministry?" Ananias asked.

"I wanted to help people, and I wanted to win souls for Christ."

"I had the same ambition you had when I was your age. I was filled with so much passion for the Word of God and God's people that I wanted to shout it everywhere I went. Pretty soon I found myself behind the pulpit preaching, and over the years, I've tried to do as much damage to the devil's kingdom as possible by snatching souls out of his hands and placing them in God's hands."

Ananias adjusted in his seat. "But as I sit here reflecting on my life's work, I wonder if I haven't in some ways veered off the path."

"That's just the devil. You've been a great leader."

"I don't doubt I've done some good, but if Gethsemane has grown to a place where it is dependent on me, then I'm afraid that Gethsemane is in an unhealthy environment. I serve the people of Gethsemane; the people do not serve me."

"Where's this coming from? Has God told you to step down?" Timothy questioned.

"No, I will leave that up to God, but when my time does come, the ministry has to be handed over to someone who is more concerned with connecting to the people than entertaining them."

Timothy smiled and nodded his head. He then returned his eyes to the chessboard.

"Have you thought about what we talked about the other day?" Ananias asked.

"I haven't really been able to think about anything else. You really threw a curve ball at me!"

"You mean God; I was just being obedient. You're more qualified than you think. You graduated from the minister's class. You know your Word, and you have a genuine love for people."

"I don't see how I can juggle being a language arts teacher by day and a pastor at night."

"I wouldn't ask you to do something that didn't require faith."

"Well, what about Pastor Childs?"

"He's a dynamic speaker, but that's not enough. You said it yourself—he's barely around. What this ministry needs is someone whose heart is intertwined with the congregation, and that's you, Timothy. You have all the makings of a great pastor. The only thing that stands in your way is this." Ananias tapped Timothy on the forehead. "You get this"—he pointed to his head—"in line with this,"—he pointed to his heart—"and God will do some amazing things in your life."

"I don't want to fail, and I don't want to let you down or bring shame to the church."

"You fail when you're afraid to risk failure in pursuit of your God-given purpose. I left a good job to take over Gethsemane. Everybody thought I was crazy, but those same people are still in the same place they were in when I left them, and God has blessed me ever since. Don't miss your chance."

A few moments passed before Timothy leaned back in his seat as if he had just remembered something important. "I'll pray on it some more"

"He'll give you clarity," Ananias told him.

Timothy left Ananias alone to ponder both the game and the conversation.

"Lord, I believe you put it in my heart to give the ministry over to Timothy. I just hope that I haven't scared him off."

CHAPTER SEVEN

Constance hit the snooze button several times before she finally got out of bed. It was Sunday, and she could not afford to miss church. That would arouse suspicion, and too many questions would follow. She managed to gather enough strength to drag herself out of bed.

The water pressure from her shower eased some of the tension in her muscles. After she adjusted the temperature from hot to lukewarm, Constance placed her head underneath the showerhead and allowed the water to run through her hair as she inhaled her violet-scented body wash.

She folded her arms and leaned forward against her peach-colored shower tile. While the water flowed down her back, she thought about the pressure behind her sophomore album and how she did not have the heart to tell Kevin that she did not want to finish the album. The devil had waited for that empty moment in the shower to plant his seeds in Constance's mind.

You are a murderer. God hates you. He's going to get you for killing your baby. So much for your gospel career. You have no business calling yourself a Christian.

Constance could not rid herself of these thoughts, nor could she hold back the tears.

"God, how could you let this happen?" Constance said.

God does not love you. You're all alone.

Constance turned off the shower and slid back the fiberglass shower door.

She wrapped a hot pink towel around her chest and a second towel around her head. She walked over and opened the medicine cabinet. She grabbed her pain medication, unscrewed the cap, put two pills in her mouth, and swallowed without water.

Constance went into the kitchen and removed a bowl of oatmeal from the microwave. She went back into the bathroom and took a few bites before she got dressed. She practiced her smiles, from the smile where no teeth showed to the smile where only the top set showed to the big smile that revealed both. Constance chose the smile where the top teeth showed because the no-teeth smile gave off a sense of trouble, while the big smile was too fake. After a few minutes of practice, she leaned in on the mirror.

"Okay, God, I promise that if you forgive me, then I'll never make the mistake of getting pregnant again. I'm sorry, Lord. I know you expect better from me."

Timothy stood outside of Gethsemane and pondered how Gethsemane Community Church did not look like a church seen in movies or in paintings. It was not a cathedral that could be seen from a distance. It was not made of stone, and it did not have a rich history.

The church stood in between a sheet metal manufacturer and a carpet factory.

Timothy's watch read 10:30 AM. He waited on the steps of the church and greeted the latecomers. There were no clouds to block the sun, so Timothy stood in its path to keep warm.

Constance still had not returned his phone call, which left him to draw the conclusion that she might have misinterpreted it. He could not afford the situation being escalated out of control, so he stood outside and waited for Constance to show up. Minutes later, he watched as her silver BMW pulled into a nearby parking spot. From a distance, everything seemed okay as Constance got out of the car and began to walk briskly toward the church. Timothy felt sort of foolish that he had overreacted; he might have freaked the young girl out.

"Sister Anderson," he called out.

"Good morning, Pastor Wells," Constance replied as she approached him.

"Did you get my message?"

"I did, but I haven't been feeling well this past week. Sorry I didn't return your call."

"I understand. Glad to see you doing better."

"Thank you," Constance said.

"Listen, the other day I was praying, and the Lord put it on my heart to pray for you. I got the feeling that something was wrong." Timothy noticed the shift in Constance's body language. Her eyes rotated from left to right.

"My sister has actually been going through a rough time with her baby daddy, so I've been lifting her up in prayer. It gets overwhelming sometimes, carrying other people's burdens."

"You and your sister must be very close," Timothy said.

"We're very close."

"Well, you know God answers prayer, so I'll be sure to pray for your sister."

Constance flashed a smile with no teeth. "Thank you, Pastor Wells." She started to walk away, but Timothy spoke again.

"Oh yeah, I've been meaning to talk with you about a possible gospel concert," Timothy said.

"What does Pastor think?" Constance asked.

"I haven't talked to him yet, but I wanted to talk with you first and see if you think that it'll be a good idea," Timothy said.

"That sounds like a great idea."

"Great. I will be in contact with you sometime this week."

"Sounds good," Constance replied. The expression on her face was as if she were asking for permission to leave.

"Well, let me not hold you up any longer." Timothy moved to the side to let Constance walk into the building.

Constance walked through the church doors, but hesitated to walk into the sanctuary as she read the sign above the doorpost, which read: ENTER THE GATES WITH THANKSGIVING AND PRAISE.

"Hey, girl!"

She turned around and Kim, her friend, walked up to her. Her round stomach poked out in her maternity clothes. Constance almost mistook Kim's wide smile for a glow, and her husband, Daryl, was right next to her with an equally wide smile.

"Hey, girl!" Constance said.

"How you been, superstar?"

"You know, hard at work." Constance rubbed her neck.

Kim went into her purse and handed Constance a small green envelope. "I wanted to invite you to my baby shower on the fourth of November."

"That's two weeks from now," Constance said.

"I know it's short notice, but I would really love it if you could come."

"Girl, I would love to come, but my schedule has been crazy with the pressure of the second album."

"You don't need to explain, but if you're in the mood for some good food, then give your girl a call."

"I will. Thank you so much, and keep me in prayer."

"We will."

Constance felt a frigid hand on her back and a chill went through her body. She turned around and saw Pastor Ananias Jones. Constance's blood warmed at the sight of him. With skin as black as berries and his head completely bald, she found him to be a very attractive older man.

Constance loved his sad, puppy-dog brown eyes, and the way his cheeks formed lines when he smiled.

"Good morning, Sister Anderson," Pastor Jones said.

"Good morning, Pastor Jones."

"It's great to see you this morning. I've been praying to the Lord that the Lord's favor will shine upon you and your album," Pastor Jones said.

Constance's smile revealed her full set of teeth. "Really?"

"Yes, so you could sing my favorite song. I know that's selfish of me to ask you something last minute, but I would really love to hear you sing."

"I don't know, Pastor. I don't feel very well."

Ananias's smile decreased, and though Constance was in no mood to sing, she did not want to disappoint her pastor.

"On second thought, I'll sing," Constance obliged.

"You don't have to. I'll understand."

"No, I want to," she insisted.

"Thank you, child!"

Ananias patted Constance on the back and proceeded to walk back to his office. Constance was almost compelled to tell him what she had gone through, but she did not want to disappoint her pastor. Instead, Constance walked up to the usher who wore the traditional black and white outfit with white gloves.

"Are there any seats toward the front?" Constance asked.

"Let me see." The usher scanned the nearly full sanctuary and held up her index finger. She got the attention of a female usher near the entrance door. The usher walked up and down the aisle, found a seat, and motioned for Constance to follow her.

"Follow her." The usher extended her hand.

"Thank you," Constance said.

Constance walked toward the female usher, who stood near the front of the sanctuary, and arrived at the third aisle. Sister Beverly, a heavyset woman with a ridiculously large hat, waved at Constance.

"Well, how are you, Sister Anderson?" Sister Beverly asked.

Constance flashed the smile that revealed her top set of teeth. "I'm fine. God bless you."

Constance slid her way toward the middle of the row. She placed her purse on an open seat and adjusted her peach-colored blazer. James sat at the drums, and her demeanor changed at the sight of him. She thought he was so fine with his bronze skin and bald head.

James spotted Constance, and after a quick flash of a smile, he turned his head to the front of the sanctuary where the praise team stood. The congregation was singing the slow-tempo song called "I Worship Because of Who You Are."

Constance received a tap on her shoulders and saw a tall man with caramel skin wearing a navy blue pinstripe suit.

"Excuse me, sister," the gentleman said.

Constance pressed her calves against the pew and the gentleman brushed past her. The gentleman held the hand of a beautiful little girl with golden brown skin and hazel eyes like hers. She wore a black velvet dress with black patent leather shoes.

The little girl waved at Constance. Constance shifted her focus back to the center of the pulpit.

Surrounded by white walls, the stage formed a half-circle with the pulpit in the middle. The song ended, and Timothy walked up to the pulpit.

"Praise the Lord, saints," Timothy said.

"Praise the Lord," the congregation said in perfect unison.

"It's good to be in the house of the Lord." Timothy's voice annoyed Constance. He sounded snotty for her taste.

"The scripture will be taken from Psalms 1."

Timothy read Psalms 1 in an almost lecture-like manner, but Constance did not even bother to open up her Bible. She was familiar with the passage.

Afterward, Timothy walked to the far right side of the stage and sat next to Pastor Jones. The choir entered from the door on the side behind the musicians' stand and filtered themselves through the four pews positioned behind the pulpit.

The choir wore burgundy gowns with the church's initials stitched in red. Mike, a short, high-yellow brother with a baby afro, walked to center stage and turned his back to the congregation. As the choir director, Mike started to wave his hands back and forth as the choir sang "Glory to Glory," an up-tempo song. Many people in the sanctuary stood up and sang along.

Mike pointed his index finger in the air, and the song reached its crescendo. When it concluded, the choir sat down, and Timothy walked back up to the pulpit.

"Praise the Lord, saints," Timothy repeated.

"Praise the Lord," half the congregation replied.

"We will now hear a selection from our very own Constance Anderson." Timothy looked out among the sanctuary for Constance, who, the pastor had informed him, would be blessing the church in song.

Constance's stomach began to turn. She gripped the seat in front of her and stood up. With legs like Jell-O, she slid across the pew and made her way down the center aisle. Timothy helped her up the two steps to the stage and handed her the microphone.

Constance had the attention of nearly four hundred people. This sight did not ease the tension in her stomach, and her two-inch heels felt unstable. She took a long, hard look at James, then she looked back at the congregation. Her throat dried up as she opened her mouth.

"Praise the Lord, saints," Constance said.

"Praise the Lord," a handful of congregants said.

Constance cleared her throat. "Excuse me. I give honor to God and my pastor, Pastor Jones. I know that sometimes trials and tribulations can get us down, but that is why we need to turn to God, because He has the answer. That's why this song is entitled 'Make Me Over Again,' and I pray that you receive these words and let them resonate within your spirit. God bless you."

Constance placed her head down and straightened out the microphone's cord. She closed her eyes and tried to remember the words to Pastor Jones's favorite song.

Associate Pastor Dennis Childs provided the accompaniment on his keyboard. Constance felt goose bumps all over her body as she began to internalize the words of the song.

The song talked about forgiveness and a fresh start. Her eyes could no longer hold back the tears, only this time when she cried, she felt relief from the pain. But she knew her relief was only for a moment.

CHAPTER EIGHT

He should have been dead, but there were two things that Darius never left home without: his gun and his bulletproof vest. The other night, his vest absorbed two shots to the chest. Upon release from county jail on suspicion of drug trafficking with a court date for Monday, Darius wasted no time in his quest for revenge.

He drove around in the black Dodge Charger he had bought Marshall for his birthday. He had one hand on the wheel and the other on his back-up glock. His whole crew's blood was stained on the concrete, and Darius could not let their deaths be in vain.

He went by the spot where the boy with the black hat hustled, and the block was emptied. Darius could not fathom that this hot spot was a ghost town, so he decided to go by his old neighborhood. Maybe they had already moved in on his territory.

Darius arrived back at Fourteenth and Williams Street. The yellow caution tape connected from the gate of the Candlewoods Apartments to a palm tree. There were no fiends, no hustlers, and no sign of his enemies. He stood underneath thick, gray clouds that brightened the caution tape. A cold chill went throughout Darius's body as he examined the crime scene. All Darius saw was dried blood and an invitation to a church; the same invitation the back of his own pants. Darius removed the invitation in and recognized the address to the church. He then placed the card in his blue Yankees jacket. He replayed the scene in his mind and could not understand how he had survived.

Darius always prided himself on being a soldier and being ready to ride or die, but when he arrived at the crime scene, his anger subsided and his sense of his own mortality ensued. He felt around to his back pocket and pulled out a crumpled up invitation with an address to Gethsemane Community Church.

CHAPTER NINE

The sweat from his neck drenched his collar. His hands shook. The only place he found sanctuary from the pain was in the Bible. Ananias likened the word of God to a punch in the rib cage. Though it stung, one could not help but to respect it for its power. His air came up short and his heart remained in a constant state of panic. He jumped at the sound of a knock on his door.

"Enter," Ananias said.

Timothy poked his head through the door. "Need anything, Pastor?"

"No, thank you. I'm fine."

Ananias searched for a Kleenex to wipe the sweat from his forehead.

"You sure?"

"Yes. Now, I need to finish my sermon."

"Okay." Timothy hesitated a moment before closing the door.

Ananias took a deep breath. "Lord Jesus, I ask right now that you allow your servant to preach one more sermon so that I may win more souls for you. In Jesus' name I pray.

Amen." Ananias stood up, straightened his tie, grabbed his Bible, and exited his office.

Ananias looked into the nearly full congregation. In the midst of blank stares and yawns, a few sat in anticipation of the Word of God. No blood flowed through his legs. Ananias held onto the pulpit for support.

He scanned over the congregation once more. Faces started to become familiar: couples he had counseled through rocky marriages, babies he had baptized, ex-addicts and friends he used to play cards with for hours.

"Thank you, Lord!" Ananias said with tears in his eyes. "Praise the Lord, saints!"

"Praise the Lord," the congregation replied

"The Word of God can be found in the book of Ezekiel. A familiar passage, but I'm sure that we will nonetheless be blessed." Ananias never grew tired of the sound of Bible pages turning.

"The other day, I had the misfortune of watching the doctors try to revive a young man. His name was Deshawn and he was only fifteen. Unfortunately, we read about Deshawn every day; young people who constantly gamble with their lives. So much so that I am afraid of the future."

Ananias had seized the attention of the entire congregation. Parents who either lost their children, or lived in daily fear that they might lose their children through random acts of violence, hung onto his every word. He also connected with the youth who had attended candlelight vigils for their fallen classmates.

"The prophet Ezekiel found himself in the land of dry bones, and the Lord asked him if the bones could live again. After all that Ezekiel had witnessed with his two eyes, he gave an honest and sincere answer. 'Lord, only you know that!' And God told the prophet to speak as he began to speak; life began to return onto the once dry bones.

"Church, I stopped by to tell you today that I speak life into a dead situation so that the dry bones of Silicon Valley can live once again. So that our children can grow up in an environment free of fear."

The majority of the congregants jumped to their feet in excitement. The warm blood flowed through his veins. Ananias's adrenaline allowed him to persevere through the pain. He managed to even give a little hop from the excitement. He sweated profusely, but to the untrained eye, he was his regular self. A sharp pain shot through his leg, and his knees buckled. He gripped the pulpit tighter, afraid that he might fall over and off the stage. He managed to gather enough strength to continue and conclude his sermon.

"The Lord wants to revive you; the Lord wants to restore you. All you have to do is answer. If there is anybody here who wants restoration, who needs God to speak life into his or her situation, I want you to come forth. We are ready to pray with you."

Ananias grabbed his drenched handkerchief and tried to wipe the sweat from his forehead. A few drops crept into his eyes and caused a burning sensation. A line of people assembled in front of the pulpit, and one by one, people in the congregation began to walk up and receive prayer. Ananias scanned the crowd. He observed a young man in a blue Yankees jacket. He was at the far left corner of the sanctuary in tears. He rocked back and forth in his chair until he finally got up and walked to the front of the congregation. Timothy prayed for him.

"Praise God! One more for the kingdom," Ananias shouted.

After the mellow music subsided and everyone returned to their seats, Ananias gave the microphone to Timothy and began his slow journey back to his office. He shifted all of his weight on his right arm, which was pressed against the banister for support, and walked down the steps of the stage. Terrified that he could fall at any moment, the relatively short distance between the stage and the pulpit seemed great and vast. Ananias took slow but sizeable steps and smiled all the way so that he would not draw too much attention to himself.

When he reached the first pew, he felt joy because he could use the edge of each pew to support him as he headed back to his office.

Ananias arrived at the doorway to be greeted by the ushers. His vision blurred at the sight of his office door at the end of the hallway.

"Lord Jesus, give me strength!" he pleaded.

Ananias felt tiny arms wrap around him, and when he looked down, there was Kala, a preteen that Ananias had christened when she was a baby, with a big smile that revealed her gap teeth.

"Hey, precious."

"You're sweaty," Kala said with a sour look on her face.

"I'm sorry. I sweat easily."

As Ananias took a step, Kala did not release her grip. They walked together, and Ananias felt a little embarrassed that a little girl was supporting him.

"You been good in school?" he made small talk.

"Yeah! I'll bring you my report card next week. Remember you promised five dollars for every A?"

"Five dollars? I think the deal was three dollars per A." Ananias grabbed his chest.

"Nope, you said five," Kala said.

"We'll have to see then."

Before he knew it, Ananias had arrived at his office. "Thank you, Jesus. Well, I have to go in here and rest."

"Okay."

"Give your momma a kiss on the cheek for me."

"Okay," Kala repeated as she skipped back into the sanctuary.

"What I wouldn't give for that kind of energy."

Ananias entered his office, but did not close his door all the way. His head started to spin, and the pain in his chest was unbearable. He almost fell on top of his desk. He collapsed in his seat and grabbed a pen. He began to write on a yellow legal note tablet. The pen faded before Ananias could completely finish his message. He searched for another pen, but became weak. His heart felt like it would explode from the pressure.

He found a pen, but it slipped out of his hands and fell onto the ground. Ananias did not have the strength to pick up the pen. He barely had his request written down before he fell out of his chair, leaving the note that read:

I want to give the church over to Timothy . . .

AFTER THE BENEDICTION

CHAPTER TEN

Dennis arrived home from work with a desire for a warm shower and a home-cooked meal.

"How was dinner?" Dennis asked his wife, Renee.

"It was fine. The kids ate and I put them to bed." Renee crossed her arms. "I couldn't make the chicken because I didn't have enough seasoning."

"How come you didn't call me while I was out?" Dennis glanced at Renee. "I would've picked some up for you."

"I did, but your phone was off."

"That must've been when I was in a meeting." Dennis sat on his cucumber green couch. His shoulders felt like he had just removed two seventy-five-pound bags of sand. The balls of his feet were tender and the callouses on his hands made it difficult for him to make a fist.

Dennis picked up the mail and separated the letters from the advertisements. He tossed the advertisements back on the coffee table, between the glass candy jar filled with Hershey's Kisses and a stack of magazines. With the exception of the cable bill, he placed the other letters on his lap. He opened the cable bill.

"The cable bill is high this month," Dennis said.

"I watched a few movies." Renee stared down at her toes.

Dennis turned the bill over and held it up for Renee to see. "This says you ordered six movies."

"I don't know how many I ordered." Renee ran her fingers through her hair.

Dennis put the bill on the coffee table. "Must be nice!" He glanced up at Renee wearing her usual baby blue T-shirt and gray sweats. Renee had purchased a certain skin product online that caused an allergic reaction. Permanent brown spots stained some parts of her face. The product ruined her caramel skin, but at times, her deep imprinted dimples made up for the defect. With the right makeup treatment, the spots were not visible; only behind closed doors did she unveil her dark secret. Dennis thought that it was monstrous to hold such a horrific thing against Renee, but he could not help but feel somewhat physically detached from his wife.

"Well, your dinner is in the microwave," Renee said.

"All right, I'll get it in a second. " Dennis looked up, and Renee had her hand on her hip, a sign that she was irritated. "What?"

"Nothing!" Renee folded her arms.

"Renee, I'm not in the mood. I've had a long day, so tell me what's up."

"Dana called today."

Dennis knew that Dana's phone call would push dinner back at least an hour. Dana and Renee both ran Sunday school, and her departure from Gethsemane had a profound effect on Renee's temperament.

"What was she calling for?"

"She's leaving Gethsemane."

"That's unfortunate," was Dennis's reply.

"A lot of people are leaving," Renee added. "It's because of the preaching now."

Dennis's head started to throb at the mere mention of church. He leaned back on the couch and rubbed his eyes with the palms of his hands. "I know a lot of people are leaving. I found out the other day that the Mitchells are leaving too," Dennis said.

"Pretty soon you'll be able to hear a pin drop at Gethsemane. It's a darn shame too." Renee shook her head.

"Don't say that!"

"What? It's the truth."

"You don't know that. Let's just wait to see what God is going to do."

"Are you planning to not talk about this?" Renee asked

"There's nothing to talk about. What's done is done."

"So what are you going to do?"

"Nothing!"

"Nothing?" Renee unfolded her arms.

"There's nothing I can do. Timothy taking over as head pastor was a decision handed down from Ananias," Dennis said.

Renee pulled her hair back behind her shoulders. She reached in her left pocket and pulled out a black hair scrunchy. She slid the scrunchy halfway on her left hand as she put her hair into a ponytail.

"And what does that say about your years of service?" Renee started in. "After all that you sacrificed for that church so that Ananias could give his life's work over to a kid; an inexperience kid on top of that!"

"He's a decent preacher," Dennis said.

"Oh, please. It takes more than that to be a pastor. It takes leadership. What congregation is going to follow a pastor that's at least ten years younger than them?"

"He has potential." Dennis shrugged.

"And you have experience. We all thought you were next

in line. You've been with this ministry for eleven years. There is no one more qualified to take over this ministry than you."

That fact alone ate away at Dennis on the inside. He put on a good show of humility, but inside, he wanted nothing more than to be pastor, and the board's announcement of Timothy as pastor was a slap in his face. But what made it worse was that Timothy's promotion came in part because of a large endorsement by Ananias.

"He has to do what the Spirit of God is leading him to do, and if that means Timothy taking over as senior pastor, then that's God's will. He may not look like a pastor, but neither did David look like a king," Dennis reasoned.

"Don't preach to me!" Renee walked over to the love seat and sat down. "Who knows what mindset Ananias was in when he made that decision? And since he's been discharged from the hospital, no one has seen him."

"Why are you so upset about this?" Dennis asked.

"Why aren't you upset?" Renee retorted.

"You complain enough as it is that I don't spend enough time with you and the kids. You want to add being a pastor of a church on top of that?"

"At least I know that you would be happy instead of moping around pretending to be humble. I'm the only person in that church who knows it gets to you to sit there Sunday after Sunday, wishing you was in that pulpit."

Dennis stood up and tried to walk away, but Renee stepped in front and pushed him.

"What do you want me to do?" Dennis threw his arms up.

"I want us to leave."

"I'm not leaving," Dennis said.

"I'm not staying." Renee leaned back and crossed her arms.

"What did you say?" Dennis walked closer to Renee.

"I'm not going to sit here and watch you continue to kill yourself for a bunch of ingrates."

"You'll do as I say." Dennis pointed at Renee.

"Or else what?" Renee poked her finger into Dennis's chest.

Dennis yanked Renee closer to him. "Woman, I'm not in the mood! Unless you want me to go to jail tonight, don't touch me!"

"Let go of me!"

Dennis released his grip, and Renee stabbed him in his back with her fingernails as he walked toward the keyboard next to the cobblestone chimney.

"That's right, walk away. That's what you're good at doing. You can't stand and face anything," Renee said.

Dennis began to play a slow melody in an effort to regain control of his emotions and drown out Renee's raspy voice. Her words felt like needles being inserted into his brain.

"Let me go to the board and talk to them. They can override Ananias's decision," Renee suggested.

"Do you know how crazy that sounds?" Dennis asked.

"They know that there are a lot of people that would follow you if you started your own church. The board won't let Timothy destroy Ananias's legacy."

"I'm not leaving unless God tells me to leave." He closed his eyes and began to play "Amazing Grace." He visualized an eagle perched on a mountain, prepared to take flight. Renee slammed her hands on the keys and interrupted the image.

"You're not going to ignore me!" she shouted.

Dennis yanked her hands off the keyboard. "Stop it!"

Renee pounded her hand on the middle of the keys. This time, Dennis knocked her hand away. "I said stop it!"

Renee tried a third time and Dennis jumped up and made his way around the keyboard. Dennis pushed Renee against the wall. He wrapped his hands around her frail throat and punched the wall next to her head.

A sharp pain shot through his hand. Dennis reveled in the fact that he evoked fear in his wife.

"Dad!" Elijah said from the end of the hallway, still in his bedtime clothes.

"Go back to bed, honey; everything is okay," Renee said with a cracked voice.

Elijah did not move, and at this moment, Dennis was more terrified than both Renee and his son. "Did you hear your mother? Go back to bed."

Dennis loosened his grip and Renee wrestled his hand away. She rushed over to Elijah and gave him a kiss on the cheek before she escorted him into the room. Like a fugitive with only seconds before the police knocked down the door, Dennis grabbed his keys and his coat and ran out of the house.

Dennis sat on one of the park benches at Caesar Chavez Park with an empty can of beer in his hand. The park was nestled in the heart of downtown San Jose. It was surrounded by neon signs, hotels, and restaurants where the incessant jazz music filled the air. He sat and observed the burgundy haze that blended with the night.

Timothy was not the first person Dennis called, but Timothy was the only person who answered the phone at 11:24 PM. Dennis figured that if Timothy left his house right after he got off the phone with him, then he should be at the park by now regardless of if he took the 101 or the 87 Interstate.

His wife held him up, or maybe he got into an accident. Calling him was probably an even bigger mistake. I should leave.

Dennis stood up to leave as he heard a car door slam. Timothy made his way toward Dennis. Timothy got closer, and Dennis hid the can of beer underneath his bench and quickly threw a couple of breath mints into his mouth. Timothy walked with a swagger, as if he were the most anointed man on the planet. Dennis regretted that he even called him.

"What's going on, Dennis?" Timothy shook Dennis's hand.

"I'm sorry for calling you so late and waking you up. I just needed someone to talk to."

"You didn't wake me. I was grading papers for my class. Why? What's going on?" Timothy asked.

"I've royally messed up," Dennis confessed.

"Okay, how?"

"My wife . . . I love her and all, but sometimes she says the wrong thing and doesn't know when to quit."

"I know what you mean," Timothy said.

"This time I snapped, and I pushed her against the wall and punched the wall. I knew that I wasn't going to hit her; I love her too much. I just wanted to scare her, but I pushed her in front of my son."

Dennis averted his eyes from Timothy for both shame and the tears welling in his eyes. "I don't want my son to think that he has an abusive father."

"You're going to have to talk with him so that he understands that what happened was a mistake." Timothy pointed at Dennis's chest.

"It seems like all we do is argue over finances." Dennis paced back and forth. "That and the demands of the job. I mean, I got a lot on my plate."

"I feel you; I'm having a hard time balancing work, family, and ministry. Emerald and I bump heads on many occasions, but I try to remember that even when she's nagging, it's out of love."

"I know, I know," Dennis said as he allowed Timothy's words to sink into his heart and hope to resonate. He looked back up at the sky with relief from his sin thanks to an unlikely source. "I love to come here sometimes at night."

"I love to come here during the jazz festival. Their catfish is off the chain," Dennis said.

"Oh, I love the catfish too," Timothy agreed.

"Thank you for coming."

"You don't have to thank me. We're brothers. Don't hesitate." He turned and faced him. "Listen, Dennis, I've been meaning to talk with you. Despite the rumor, I did not lobby for this position. I'm was certain that Ananias would name you as his successor if anything happened."

"You don't have to explain. Ananias has unquestionable integrity. I trust his judgment. You're an anointed minister with a bright future ahead of you."

"We've sustained a massive loss in membership. I'm going to need dedicated and faithful men of God like yourself to help rebuild."

"To be honest with you, Pastor, I've been doing a lot of thinking, and maybe it's time for me to strike out on my own and start my own ministry," Dennis said smugly.

"Have you heard from God?"

"Of course I've heard from God!" Dennis cringed at the fact that he had lied to his pastor.

"Well, I know that God will bless your ministry," Timothy said.

"I'm not leaving yet, but just so you know, I have given it some thought."

Timothy shook Dennis's hand. "I understand. You got to do what the Lord is calling you to do."

"Thank you again," Dennis said.

On the way home, instead of reconciliation with his wife, Cecilia dominated Dennis's thoughts, and his desire for her grew.

CHAPTER ELEVEN

Vernon sat alone in the classroom. The frame of the man at the chalkboard resembled his uncle. He did not turn around; he just continued to write. The chalk pierced the chalkboard, forming the sentence: I will not tell.

Vernon ran for the door, but could not open it no matter how hard he twisted the knob. On the other side of the window, a swarm of people walked by, but he could not get their attention no matter how hard he banged on the window. Vernon screamed and felt a jolt in his throat, but nothing came out. Instead, he only heard the sound of the chalk against the chalkboard, until his alarm clock went off.

At home, Vernon crept around like a spy. At twelve years old, he walked softly with decrepit posture. His mom would often call out to him from a different part of the house just to make sure that he was still home.

At school, the girls laughed and giggled at the sight of him, while the boys called him gay and other derogatory names as they threw him into the girls' locker room. His four-year-old sister, Autumn, always walked into his room unannounced with a toy in her hands.

"Let's play," she said this morning, like normal.

"It's too early, Autumn. I have to finish this paper," Vernon told her.

Autumn did not take no for an answer. She pulled on Vernon's arm. "Come on. Play with me."

"I promise when I get home today, we'll play, but I have to finish."

The second denial caused Autumn to walk away with a fat bottom lip and her head down. Vernon went back to his work, an essay on a poem by Langston Hughes that was due for his favorite teacher, Mr. Wells. He completed the essay last night, but wanted to give it one last review and to stare at the posters on his wall. Vernon had pictures of 50 Cent, LL Cool J, and Tyrese. All of the men on the posters wore a white or black tank top. He admired them for their sculptured bodies because the mirror reflected his worthless, dull, black skin and his malnourished body.

"Mom wants you in the kitchen." Autumn ran back into the room almost out of breath.

"All right," Vernon said after he let out a sigh.

Autumn ran back out of Vernon's room, and he followed her into the kitchen. Her shoes squeaked against the kitchen tile. Vernon's mother, Kristal, was always mistaken as his big sister. She stood at the sink and rinsed raw chicken before she pulled the skin off and placed the rest in a bag of flour.

"You wanted to see me?" Vernon asked his mother.

"Greg and I are going to Monterey for the weekend, so you and your sister are going over your Uncle Alex's," Kristal said with her back turned.

"I don't want to go over my Uncle Alex's house." Vernon shook his head, and the bass in his voice dropped.

Vernon's mom turned around with an awkward look on her face. Vernon did not like it when his mom made ugly faces.

"Boy, I know you done lost your mind talking to me that way."

Kristal's voice sent a shock wave through Vernon's body, but Vernon held his ground. "Mom, I really don't want to go over Uncle Alex's."

"He told me that you've been cutting up lately, and he has to tell you more than once to settle down."

"He's lying, Mom. He's lying. Please don't make me go back to my uncle's house! Please, Mom, I'll do whatever you want, just don't let my sister go, or me," Vernon said, unable to hold back the tears.

"Boy, what's wrong with you? Crying like a little girl? Now, you stop crying and tell me why you don't want to go over your uncle's house."

Satan saw his opportunity. *Don't tell. He'll hurt your sister, and it will be all your fault, and your mother would never forgive you.*

In Vernon's mind, he could not afford to put his family at risk. His uncle made a strict warning that if Vernon said a word, then something would happen to Autumn.

"Fine then, if you don't want to tell me, then that's on you, but unless you tell me, you're going to your uncle's house on Saturday."

Vernon's tears did not stop. Kristal continued to prepare dinner, and Vernon returned to his room. He contemplated suicide, but could not figure out anything that could make his death painless. But what could be more painful than living?

CHAPTER TWELVE

In all honesty, Emerald did not feel like the First Lady. She remained the church secretary and kept close watch over the daily affairs of the church. Timothy came in after school for meetings and counseling, and Emerald enjoyed being able to spend more time with her husband, even if they only talked about ministry.

Emerald surveyed Timothy's new office. A picture of Ananias and the Mayor of San Jose hung on the wall. There was a plaque on the wall that read: SPECIAL RECOGNITION OF PASTOR ANANIAS JONES FOR ALL OF HIS YEARS OF SERVICE. The bookshelf did not change, and Ananias's old worn, rusty brown leather chair remained in Timothy's new office. Timothy did manage to place a wedding photo of him and his wife on the desk and change the nameplate.

"Babe, Pastor Lewis called regarding the revival this Friday," Emerald said.

Timothy stood up and sorted through a handful of papers.

"That's right; Pastor was supposed to preach the revival on the twelfth. That's two days from now. Call Pastor Lewis and tell him that I'm available to preach the revival if he needs me."

"Actually, he called to tell me that they found a replacement. Pastor Harris from New Life will preach. But he wanted me to tell you that he's praying for you, and he knows that God's blessing is upon the ministry."

"Well, praise God that Pastor Harris was able to come in on such short notice. I'm sure he'll bring an awesome Word."

Timothy examined the stacks of papers on his desk and opened books, then collapsed into his chair. Without hesitation, Emerald went over to Timothy and wrapped her arms around him. She kissed the top of his head and then placed the right side of her face on top of his head. Timothy rubbed his wife's forearm.

"Don't worry, baby. People know you have a lot on your plate, and they see that. God wants you to get the ministry in order," Emerald comforted her husband.

"You're right," Timothy said after he let out a deep breath.

Emerald began to massage Timothy's shoulders. "Come on now, you got an appointment session with Jamyla."

"I also got Bible study tonight!"

"I know. Maybe you should talk about seed time and harvest. People don't seem to get tired of hearing about that."

"I know. Thanks, babe." He kissed her on the cheek.

Emerald left Timothy's office and found Jamyla in the lobby. She wore a dark brown suit that Emerald liked.

"She must have man issues," Emerald said under her breath.

"Good morning, First Lady," Jamyla stated.

"Girl, please, it's still Emerald."

"It's weird seeing you as First Lady," Jamyla relayed.

"God's ways are mysterious." Emerald shrugged her shoulders.

"Is Pastor in?"

"Yes, he'll be in with you in a second."

"Okay," Jamyla took a seat.

The door of her husband's office opened, and Timothy walked briskly and extended his hand to Jamyla.

"Thank you for your patience. I know you're very busy," Timothy said

"I'm just grateful that you're able to see me on such short notice." Jamyla stood.

"I won't hold you two up." Emerald walked back to her office. She stopped at the doorway and watched Jamyla follow Timothy into his office and close the door. She became uneasy about what might occur on the other side of the door. Before Gethsemane, Emerald had attended Mt. Zion, a prominent church that suffered a scandal which involved the pastor and a woman he counseled. Emerald never questioned Timothy's fidelity. As silly as it may sound, Emerald could tell by the way he kissed and embraced her that she was the only woman he desired. Her only competition for her husband's affection was his work, but even with her husband's proven track record, Emerald still felt uneasy.

Emerald decided to refocus her attention on the announcements, but she paid close attention to the clock. She wasn't sure at what time Timothy began his session with Jamyla.

Twenty minutes later, Jamyla came out of Timothy's office in tears, with tissue in hand.

"Everything okay?" Emerald asked from her desk.

Jamyla only returned a half smile. As soon as she left, Emerald headed to Timothy's office, only to find him reengaged in his work.

"What's up, babe?" Timothy looked up

"Apparently nothing," Emerald said under her breath. "I was going to get some lunch and was wondering if you want me to pick you up something?"

"Maybe sandwiches from the deli up the street," Timothy

said with his eyes full of excitement. "Oh, while you're out, could you pick up the books I have on reserve at Ethereal Bookstore? And A.S. Print Shop says that my new business cards are available."

"I am not about to spend my lunch running your errands."

"Thanks, babe." Timothy put his head back down and continued to write on his note tablet, oblivious to his wife's refusal.

Tommy's Sandwich Shop occupied a small corner of an otherwise industrial lot; they always kept busy. The line wrapped around the corner from noon until about two in the afternoon. Emerald arrived at 4:13 PM.

Two men waited beside her under the white sign designated for pick-ups. They used incessant vulgar language with a blatant disregard for the presence of a lady. One of the men Emerald recognized as a member of Gethsemane.

"Number eighty-one!" the manager called out.

Emerald held up her receipt and walked to the front of the counter to pick up a sandwich in a brown paper bag. Emerald also purchased a bag of chips and a bottle of water.

"Sister Wells!" Eric, a tall, muscular electrician who had joined Gethsemane five years ago, said.

"Hello, Eric, how are you?"

"I'm good. Just trying to get me something to eat before I have to head back to the job."

"I know that's right. Just picking up something for my husband."

"How's he doing anyway?"

"He fine, very busy with the ministry."

"I'm sure he is. It's been months since I've been. I need to start going back to church. Besides, I really miss Pastor Jones's preaching."

"Pastor Jones retired."

"For real? When?" Eric asked with his head tilted to the side.

"Almost four months ago."

"What happened?"

"He had a heart attack after one service, but he's okay."

"My God, I'm glad he's all right. So who's the Pastor now?"

"Timothy!"

Emerald recognized the bewildered look on Eric's face. Apparently, she stood alone in her opinion that Timothy possessed the fortitude to lead Gethsemane to new ground.

"Okay, well, I'm going to have to come to visit one of these days. It's just that I work on Sundays."

"I understand, but if you ever get a Sunday off, stop by."

When Emerald returned from lunch, Timothy was in the same place in which she had left him. He scribbled notes down on a note tablet and did not bother to look up when Emerald handed him his sandwich. He just took the sandwich and continued to write.

"How's it coming along?" she asked.

Timothy did not respond. He just continued to write. Normally, Emerald would take the hint, but this time she was determined to get her husband's attention, so she remained in the same spot.

"What's up, babe?" Timothy spoke.

Emerald was so irritated that she forgot her original intentions. "Babe, please put the pen down and look at me."

Timothy dropped his pen and picked his head up. Taken aback by how promptly Timothy responded to her command, Emerald searched her mind to find a coherent statement.

"Listen, I know you got a lot on your plate, and I'm so proud of how you have stepped up in the leadership position and taken the reigns."

She paused for a moment to let her words resonate. By the look on his face, she knew she had his attention.

"Thanks." Timothy reached for the pen.

"But, babe, I got to say this. I don't mean to put any more on you, but this has been bothering me for a while now."

Timothy leaned back in the chair, and his countenance changed. Emerald recognized his demeanor as one of exhaustion.

"What is it?"

"Listen, I'm still trying to make sense of what has happened. One minute I was the secretary, next minute I'm the First Lady, and this has been one huge juggling act. But with that said, in spite of the curve ball God has thrown, I've still kept what's important first, which is my family and my devotion to you as my husband."

"So you're saying I haven't?" Timothy raised his eyebrows.

"I'm not saying that."

"What are you saying?"

"I'm saying that it would be nice if we could go to lunch once in a while instead of me always bringing you lunch."

Timothy sat up and went back to writing again. "Okay, fine."

Emerald became even more irritated and refused to move. This time, it did not take long for Timothy to acknowledge his wife.

Timothy glanced up. "What's wrong now?"

"You don't get it, do you?"

Timothy fell back into his chair. "I said we'll go out to lunch."

"You said it because you want me to shut up so you can go back to work, not because you really desire to have lunch with your wife."

Timothy started to laugh, and Emerald became even more enraged that Timothy found her pain funny.

"Emerald, I don't need this right now. I got members walking out left and right. I just got off the phone with Brother

Peterson wanting me to ordain him as a pastor so he can take over a church in Wyoming. And on top of all that, I got Bible study tonight and I still don't have a topic. Now, you know I didn't ask for this, but I'm determined to see this thing through, and I need you by my side because I don't have a whole lot of people in my corner."

"Never mind then, forget it." Emerald reached back, opened the door and started to back out.

"No, wait. Tell me what you want me to do."

"I don't know!" Emerald slung her hands in the air in frustration.

"No, you do know, because you wouldn't have approached me otherwise. You wouldn't have mentioned it." Timothy leaned back in his chair and folded his hands.

"I don't know, Timothy."

"Just tell me, and I'll do it."

"I'm not going to tell you how to be a husband. You have to figure it out for yourself, just like I take the time out to find out what you need."

Emerald slammed the door behind her and stormed back to her office, only to find Mr. Blake in the hallway. Mr. Blake owned the property on which Gethsemane stood. Against his reservations, he leased the building to the church after the collapse of a dot.com that left the building vacant. He observed the pictures on the wall of past church events. Emerald knew that Blake was not on the schedule to meet with Timothy today. His appearance aroused suspicion.

"Mr. Blake, what a pleasant surprise," Emerald lied.

"Hello, Mrs. Wells. I had a gap in my schedule, and I figured that I would come by and visit."

"Does Timothy know you needed to see him?" Emerald asked.

"No, but I thought I might catch him if he had a few minutes open in his schedule."

"I'll check and see," Emerald said.

She briskly walked to Timothy's office and knocked on his door.

"Come in," Timothy called out.

Emerald walked in and closed the door behind her. "Mr. Blake is in the lobby."

"What's he doing here?" Timothy said with a perplexed look.

"He's here to see you."

Timothy looked at his desk, the signal for Emerald to make quick short stacks of papers while Timothy closed all of his books and stacked them on top of each other.

Emerald hid two of the stacks of paper in a drawer next to Timothy's desk, and then she grabbed one book from the stack, opened it and placed it on the middle of his desk.

"I'll go tell him that you will be out in a minute. Fix your tie."

"Okay!" Timothy said as he fixed his tie and unrolled his sleeves.

Emerald walked out of Timothy's office and into the lobby with more composure and control. "He'll be right out," she said.

"Okay." Mr. Blake paced the floor.

Moments later, Timothy emerged from his office. "Good to see you, Mr. Blake."

"Good to see you as well, Mr. Wells." They shook hands.

"So what brings you here?"

"I had a few minutes open in my schedule, and there were some things that I wanted to talk to you about."

"Well, we can discuss this in my office."

"Sure."

Emerald watched Timothy and Mr. Blake head into her husband's office.

For Charles Blake, time was money. No matter where he was, he always calculated whether he was gaining or losing money. He even went so far as to calculate that he made a little over fifteen cents per minute. He sat in Timothy's office with a good chance to make money.

"So, how's it going?" Blake asked.

"A little overwhelming," Timothy admitted.

"I can imagine. I remember what it was like when I started my company."

"But God is good and He will work everything out."

Blake viewed religion as training wheels for the weak-minded. He never thought anyone who believed in a higher power was intelligent. Tenacity and hard work showed more dividends in his opinion.

"Listen, Timothy, I'm not here to waste your time. I came here because, as you know, some of your members work for me at Blake's Software, and I've been hearing some unsettling news that the church might be in trouble."

"How so?" Timothy asked with his head tilted to the side.

"Well, I understand that before you took over, there was an average of about four hundred in attendance on most Sundays. I hear last week there were barely two hundred people in attendance."

"Pastor Jones was beloved not just by this church, but by the community. His retirement caused a lot of people to uproot and search for a new church."

"I know better than anyone that change can be costly, but to suffer over fifty percent loss in membership in less than four months brings up a major red flag for me."

"We've never been late on a payment."

"I understand, but you have to understand my situation. Six years ago when Ananias moved in here, he signed a seven-year contract paying seventeen cents per square foot.

"This property is now worth thirty-seven cents per square foot. I've been getting a lot of attractive offers from other companies who think this building is perfect for expanding their operations. So I have to wonder if I can continue to rent out this space to a church that, despite being exempt from paying property tax, can barely make rent. Not to mention the extra cost I have to pay in liability insurance, just for having a church on industrial property."

Blake could hear the hostility in his own voice. He knew the quickest way to end negotiations and place someone on the defense was hostility. Regardless of whether he dealt with a CEO of a Fortune 500 company or a small-time pastor, he could not afford to be abrasive.

"Mr. Blake, I understand your concerns, and I can assure you that we will uphold our end by paying rent on time," Timothy said.

"Look, Timothy, I know you got a lot hanging over your head, and I'm not trying to give you a hard time, but at the end of the day, I need to do what's best for my family. Your lease is up in April. I'm going to have to raise the rent by twenty-five hundred dollars if you decide to renew your lease."

Timothy's eyes enlarged at the news.

"I'm sorry. I don't know what to tell you," Blake said.

"I understand your situation, and we'll do our best."

Blake stood up and offered his hand to Timothy. "I wish you the best of luck."

"Thank you for your concerns, Mr. Blake."

Emerald witnessed Mr. Blake storm out of her husband's office without so much as a good-bye. She felt the kind of excitement that a person gets when they watch soap operas. She hustled to Timothy's office.

"What happened?" she asked.

"He wants us gone!" Timothy exclaimed.

"What? He's evicting us?"

"Not exactly, but he is raising our rent by twenty-five hundred dollars come April first."

"We can barely afford the eight thousand a month that

we're paying now; I can't even fathom the church being able to pay over ten thousand dollars. He can't do that!"

"He's the owner of the building. He can do whatever he wants. We have to have faith that God will work something out. We've got two months."

Emerald could tell that her husband felt defeated from the look on his face. Everything seemed to be happening all at once. "We've got time; God will work something out." Once again, Emerald began to massage Timothy's shoulders as he sat with his elbows on the desk and his face buried in his hands. "Don't stress out, babe. You know God will see us through this."

Timothy lifted his face from his hands. "I know."

He grabbed several sheets of paper that had topics and scriptures written on them. "I don't know what to speak on at tonight's Bible study."

Emerald glanced at the papers. "I definitely wouldn't do a lesson about tithing. You know how folks get when you start to talk about money."

"I was thinking of starting a series rather than doing a different topic every week."

Emerald gave the papers a second glance. "What about faith?"

"Too generic."

"You can talk about the importance of faith and give examples of the hero of faith in the Bible."

Timothy gave Emerald a look that she perceived to be an epiphany. "I could center the study on the prophets of the Bible that are highlighted in Hebrews. That's a great idea, babe."

"Well, the first story is Abel," Emerald said.

"I can talk about how Abel gave his best offering and how we need to give our best to God. That story encompasses so many aspects of our lives."

"That sounds like a good lesson," Emerald said.

Timothy got up from his desk and walked toward Emerald. "Listen, nothing that was said today fell on deaf ears. I love you, and I can't do this without you."

Timothy gently grabbed Emerald by her hand and pulled her close. He kissed her on the forehead and finished with a kiss on the lips. Emerald hugged her husband and said a silent prayer that God would grant her more patience with her husband. He needed her now more than ever.

CHAPTER THIRTEEN

Constance listened to the melody in search of the right words to blend, but was unsuccessful. Three hours had passed in the studio, and the only thing she had managed to accomplish was devouring four packs of Twinkies. The sight of the empty Twinkie wrappers on the small wooden table next to the switchboard gave her a sour taste in her mouth and almost made her heave.

She recorded her frustrations in a hot pink journal. Her journal became the only place she could vent. Even though her journal entries were very therapeutic, it didn't help her finish her album that was weeks late.

Kevin entered the room with a dozen red roses in a vase.

"Oh, how sweet!" Constance said with her hands over her mouth.

"Baby girl, I love you, but not that much," he joked. "These ain't from me." Kevin set the flowers down on the table.

Constance reached for the card. After she read it, she tossed it onto the table.

"That's not the usual response when a man send flowers," Kevin said.

Constance hadn't been to church in a couple of Sundays, so she hadn't seen James. Although she had not returned any of James's phone calls, he called at least two times a day, and now he had sent flowers.

"What's wrong with you?" Kevin asked.

She wished she could mask her pain better, but she could not. Despite her best efforts, her behavior only spawned more questions. "I can't do this anymore."

"Okay, you're going to have to be a little more specific," Kevin said with his hand on her shoulder.

"I don't know if I can do this gospel music thing anymore."

"Baby girl, you've had a lot on your plate—from work to your relationship to this album. You're probably just exhausted, and that's understandable, but we're almost done. As soon as we finish this song, that's it. We'll send this to the label and see what happens from there."

"That's what I'm trying to say; I don't even have the strength to finish a song. All I've done is sit, complain, and eat Twinkies."

"You didn't touch my cupcakes, did you?" Kevin asked with his eyes enlarged.

Constance let out a donkey type of laugh. She was embarrassed that Kevin heard it, but she could not control it. There had not been a lot of things for her to laugh about lately, so she wanted to magnify it as much as possible in hopes that she could banish all of the horrible feelings she was harboring inside.

"I'm glad you find this funny, because I don't. I got those cup cakes on a two for three dollars deal at the store," Kevin said.

The serious look on Kevin's face only made Constance laugh even more, until Kevin finally broke down and laughed with her. After a minute, the laughter settled down.

"You're an amazing woman, Constance. Don't let the devil steal your joy. We send the album to the studio on Friday.

Just give me your best effort tonight and tomorrow, and I promise you, I'll leave you alone on Friday. Can you do that for me?"

"I think I can."

Constance took Kevin's compliment with a grain of salt because he did not know the truth, and his opinion of her would change if she told him what type of woman she really was.

CHAPTER FOURTEEN

Darius turned off the stove and removed the white jar from the pot. He shook the powdery substance until it started to become solid. The more rocks that appeared, the more Darius fought back the tears. He had to decide whether to hustle or pray.

He wore the same clothes he had worn to his job interview. For the last four months, Darius had managed to attend church on several occasions, but still had troubles with fully committing to the Christian walk. His new life came with a heavy price tag. He spent the bulk of his money on lawyer fees to keep him out of prison. The judge vowed to give Darius time if he ever appeared in his courtroom again.

He knew a lot of people who got out of prison and vowed to make a change for the better only to find that society had not cancelled the so-called debt they had paid in prison. Yet, Darius pounded the pavement every day in search of work, but his arrest record prevented him from being employed.

He swung at his invisible enemies: the manager of an electronics store where Darius interviewed today and the malnourished pretender in the black cap who had shot him and murdered his crew. He had wanted revenge since day one, and Darius fought within himself not to grab his pistol and seek it.

A paradox was on his kitchen table. A Bible sat in the midst of empty plastic bottles and razors. It was the same Bible Timothy had given him. He planned to read the Bible from cover to cover, but he had only gotten to Genesis chapter five. Darius got lost somewhere in the midst of all the "begot."

"Lord, please help me to find a scripture," Darius said out loud with his Bible in his hand.

In church, Darius had listened to countless stories of people who had randomly opened their Bibles and found a scripture that spoke directly to them. Darius tried this method, but found himself in the book of Leviticus with a discussion about an animal with a split huff.

"So much for that idea." He placed his Bible on the table and collapsed onto his black leather couch. Darius turned on the TV to find two women engaged in a catfight over an unattractive guy who danced around them. He changed the channel to a music video. Half-naked girls danced in front of rappers with platinum crucifix chains and platinum grills with diamonds in them. The rappers chanted, "He ain't got more hoes than me!" to the infectious beat.

"How you gonna make a song called, 'He Ain't Got More Hoes Than Me?' That's wack!" Darius said to himself.

He changed the channel to a church service in progress in what appeared to be a conference room. A man with mascara on his face stood in front of a woman in a wheelchair.

"How long have you been in that wheelchair?" the man asked the woman.

"Forty-three years," the frail old woman replied.

"The Bible says that Jesus came to a lame person and asked him if he wanted to be healed. I am going to ask you the same thing. Do you want to be healed?"

"Yes!" the old woman cried out.

"Well, then arise and walk." The man took the woman by the hand, lifting her out of her wheelchair. A handful of people started to shout and dance. Even the once lame old woman started to dance as well. The program then cut to a segment that offered healing oil for $19.95.

"Can't knock the hustle." Darius walked back to the table and began to place the crack rocks into bottles. He reasoned that this was his only skill. "Lord, if you have a better way, please show me."

Darius examined the bottle and smiled at the fact that he could still make bottles with very little powdery residue. He loved Pastor Wells, and he had learned a lot since he had become a Christian, but church painted a picture of a world that Darius never could seem to get to. The Bible talked about patience and longsuffering, qualities that Darius did not find desirable at the moment. So for now, he had to do what he had to do.

Darius relocated to the east side of Palo Alto from San Jose as a precautionary measure. He still could not figure out how the home of Stanford University was also the home of some of the toughest thugs and drug dealers.

His Escalade was confiscated after the shooting incident, so Darius rode in the Dodge Charger. He loved the sound that came from the engine when he picked up speed. Darius could not listen to any of his gospel CDs on the drive to San Jose. He needed music that would feed his anger. He chose to listen to an underground rap CD he had held onto after he got saved.

He listened to hardcore rap to help deaden his emotions and center his thoughts on the task at hand. He drew closer to Twelfth and William Streets.

Mr. Jackson had finally replaced the broken front window

of his liquor store. Ursula, the neighborhood prostitute, held her post at the payphone as usual. Caution tape surrounded a closed sandwich shop next to the apartments where Darius used to sell drugs.

He arrived at the spot that had claimed the lives of his entire crew. A cold chill crept up Darius's body at the sight of the same tall, skinny black dude that had tried to kill him four months ago. The boy's entire crew had taken over the block, and that aggravated Darius. They were young, sloppy, and not even alert; the type of hustlers who got into the game because of the movies and music that had glorified it. Darius felt that his hand had been forced.

The desire to kill arose within him. A loaded gun in the glove compartment only increased his temptation. He pulled around the corner, but maintained a visual of the hustlers on the block. He was itching to go into his glove compartment. With the engine off, he managed not to get their attention.

Go ahead, avenge your brothers. Don't let them die in vain. God would understand. Satan taunted him.

He recalled a Bible study where Pastor Wells explored the passage about when Jesus commanded man to love his enemies. At the time, Darius had found the lesson to be profound, but now, less than a hundred feet away from his enemy, Darius could not help but to see the absurdity of the lesson. He opened the glove compartment and removed the glock. Having the glock in his hand only increased his urge to pull the trigger.

Don't be a punk! You know your boys would ride for you if it had happened to you. They murdered your whole crew and you're not going to get revenge? You're not a gangster. You're as fake as they are!

"Vengeance is mine, says the Lord. Be good to those who do evil to you. Thou preparest the table before me in the presence of my enemies," Darius said to himself.

It looks like God is taking his sweet time.

Darius banged his head against the steering wheel and shook it with both hands. He wanted to kill. The idea alone gave him a rush of adrenaline, but there was also a sense that God had spared him for a purpose—a purpose that was much greater than revenge. He tossed the gun back into the glove compartment and slammed it shut. He turned on the ignition and sped off. Darius passed by Sam, the dope fiend, still on a mission for his next fix.

"That's a darn shame." Darius shook his head.

Sam allowed crack to reduce him to a bum. He had no family to take care of him for fear that he would steal from them. He lived between fixes with an unbearable reality that awaited him on the other side of his high. Darius rolled past Sam and went up the street for several blocks before he pulled his car over and threw the drugs in a sewage drain.

CHAPTER FIFTEEN

Timothy realized he had "Saturday Night Fever." But it was not a reference to a popular movie. In the evangelical world, the term was coined for a pastor who waited until Saturday to prepare his Sunday message. With very little daylight left, Timothy felt the fever in his office as he worked on his sermon for the next day.

Ananias had taught Timothy the best way to outline his sermon. First, find the scripture, then write out an introduction. Provide definitions for the chosen title. Timothy had entitled his sermon "Avoid the Snare." He found an adequate scripture and the proper definition, but he needed a good illustration. The key to any good sermon was a good illustration. There needed to be something that brought the ancient text into modern perspective.

He felt the inside of his stomach eat away at his intestines as his strength was sapped from fasting. Timothy hoped that the power of fasting would help him to deliver a powerful sermon. As he searched through childhood memories for an illustration, he heard a knock on his door.

"Come in," Timothy said, somewhat startled.

The door cracked open partially, and Darius poked his head through the door.

"What's good with you, Pastor?"

"What a pleasant surprise. What's going on, D?" Timothy flashed a big smile.

"Nothing. I was in the neighborhood."

"Didn't you move?"

"Yeah, I stay in E.P.A. now. I just came out to visit some friends."

"I hope these aren't the friends that you were running the streets with."

"Naw, they good folks."

"Well, I'm just sitting here working on my sermon."

"Do you play?" Darius pointed to the chessboard.

Timothy turned to the chessboard with the unfinished game between him and Ananias. "Yes, I've been known to school a few people."

"I'm a beast at this game."

"Well, I think I have enough time to tame the beast." Timothy looked at his watch.

"All right, let's do this!"

Darius took a seat next to the plants, while Timothy sat next to the bookshelf. The two rearranged their pieces to the starting point.

"On you, sir," Timothy said.

Darius moved his pawn. Moments later, Timothy moved his pawn.

"How's the job search?" Timothy asked.

"It's whatever. I've had a few interviews only to be tripped up because of my record. I did a stretch in Riker's Island for possession, and that record has followed me everywhere."

"Society makes it hard for a brother to get a legitimate job when he has a prior."

"I know. I'm sitting here begging for a job paying twelve an hour. I can make ten times that hustling." Darius moved his knight.

"Yeah, but you have to deal with constantly looking over your shoulder."

"Right now, it seems worth it. I'm over here struggling, and if I'm about to get evicted from my apartment, then what am I to do? Pray?"

"Darius, I'm going to tell you something very important. Don't forfeit your destiny on account of fast money. I know the odds seem insurmountable, but when you have a worldly mindset, you're subject to all kinds of attacks. When you have God's perspective, then you know that He will take care of everything."

"And that's the thing that is hard for me to do, is trust God. I'm so used to doing it myself; to turn it over to a God I can not see is hard for me."

Timothy stared at the chessboard long enough to create awkward silence.

"You know, Pastor Jones and I played this game for count-less hours in intense theological discussions. You know what we discovered while playing this game?"

"Naw," Darius said.

"We realize that life is a chess game, and that there are an infinite number of possibilities. But no matter what choices we make in life, the end result is we either win or we lose. The key is whose strategy are you going to follow? The devil's, which appears to be the path of victory, but ultimately leads to defeat? Or God's, which may not seem like the best strat-egy, but it always guarantees victory?"

Timothy made another move and looked at his watch. "I actually got to get back to my sermon."

Darius did not move right away. Instead, he sat in the chair with his head down.

"You okay, D?"

"Pastor, I know you need to get back to your sermon, but I got something I need to get off my chest, and it's been sitting here for a while."

"What is it?"

Darius lifted his head up with bright pink eyes and his shoulders sunk in.

"Seriously, yo, you don't understand. I was the man in Jersey. I'm talking about, I could leave my car unlocked, and nobody would fool with it. I was getting mad money to the point where my cousin kept begging me to put him on, until finally I let him work the corner with me. My grandmother fought tooth and nail to keep him off the block, but it was pointless. As soon as she brought him in, he'd sneak out. Then one night, my grandmother came looking for him, and some cats sprayed the block. My grandmother was gunned down on her steps."

Darius put his head back down and Timothy's brain froze with the image of a frail grandmother on her stoop, dead.

"I spent the entire night driving around with the burner in my hand, planning to fill them up with hot lead," Darius continued. "I couldn't go home and face my family. I couldn't find the people who did it either. So finally I went to the airport and bought a ticket to get as far away from Jersey as possible. I don't know whose strategy I'm playing. If it's God's, then why did my grandmother have to die?"

Timothy leaned back in his chair and took a deep breath.

"Darius, there is a great ministry that God has birthed within you, but right now you're on dangerous ground because you're in transition from your old nature to your new nature. But I promise you that if you let God have the reins, then He'll do such an awesome work in your life that it would seem like everything that you've been through was meant to happen. Don't give up in the transition."

With tears in his eyes, Darius managed to crack a smile. "I won't, Pastor, and I feel like God does have something for me. I just need to get my scripture knowledge up."

"You don't need to know a whole lot of scripture; all you need to know is how God saved you. Your testimony is one of your strongest weapons."

"All right, Pastor."

They pounded their fists against each other as Darius left. Timothy not only got his illustration, he got a great new topic for his sermon.

A police siren sounded, then a bright white light flashed on Darius just before he entered the 280 Interstate off-ramp.

"I can't believe this." Darius stared at the glove compartment. "Lord, if you can get me out of this one, I promise I'll get rid of this gun immediately."

A flashlight tapped against his window. Darius rolled it down, and the brightness of the flashlight temporarily blinded him.

"License and registration," the officer said.

Darius turned away from the flashlight and put his hand up to deflect the beam.

"Yo, I'm here visiting my cousin. This is his car." Darius handed the officer his driver's license, which had not expired. Darius had never seen this officer before, so he figured he just might get by on his fable of being there on vacation.

"How long have you been out here?" The officer centered his light on Darius's out-of-state driver's license.

"Only a couple of days."

Another squad car pulled up behind the first police officer. Darius heard the officer get out and the car door slam behind him. It was too dark outside for Darius to make out the other officer's face.

"What do we have here?" the second officer asked.

"A car going over the speed limit." The first officer moved aside to let the second officer take a peek into the car.

Darius got a good look at the officer. It was none other than Officer Peterson, wearing a wide smile.

"What up, D? See you got a new car," Officer Peterson said.

"You know him?" the first officer asked.

"Yeah, he's one of those low-life drug dealers who sell on Twelfth and Williams Street."

"Not anymore. I got my life straight with God," Darius informed him.

"Is that right? So, did God give you this new car?" Officer Peterson asked

Darius did not respond. He just stared straight ahead and ignored Officer Peterson.

"Would you mind stepping outside of the car, sir?" the first officer asked.

Hesitantly, Darius got out of the car and Officer Peterson pounced on him, turned him against the car, and frisked him.

"You mind if we have a look in your trunk?" the first officer asked.

"You got a warrant?" Darius replied.

Officer Peterson swung Darius around and jammed his forearm into his throat. Peterson pressed forward and bent Darius into an awkward position.

"Don't get cute with us. We can search based on suspicion alone." Officer Peterson turned to his fellow officer. "Why don't you go and search that trunk, Officer Manning."

"Open the trunk," Officer Manning demanded.

Darius broke from Officer Peterson's grip and opened the trunk with his key. The trunk popped open, and Officer Manning did a thorough search.

A minute later, Officer Manning closed the trunk. "Nothing."

Officer Manning walked around the passenger's side with his flashlight. He opened the door and did a quick scan of the interior. Darius turned his back to Officer Manning. Instead, he looked across the street at a nearby liquor store. A small cluster of people went in and out.

Meanwhile, Officer Manning opened the glove compartment and removed the gun with his index finger.

"Well, look what we have here!" Officer Manning said as he held up the gun with his index finger for both Darius and Officer Peterson to see.

Officer Peterson threw Darius on the ground and twisted his arm behind his back. The cold steel of the handcuffs clamped on Darius's wrists and nearly cut off his blood circulation.

"You're under arrest for carrying a concealed weapon." Officer Peterson pushed Darius's face against the concrete and leaned into his ear. "Not even Jesus can save you now."

CHAPTER SIXTEEN

On Sunday morning when Dennis got out of bed, it became a mad dash to get ready for church in time for service.

Dennis opened the bedroom door and peeked into the kitchen where Elijah poured his cereal into a giant bowl.

"You better not waste that cereal. You better eat all of it," Dennis ordered.

"I won't," his son assured him.

Dennis found Renee in the bathroom while Jasmine played with her bath water.

"Stop splashing," Renee said.

"It's 9:32 AM," Dennis said with agitation.

"I know what time it is!" Renee avoided eye contact and continued to fix her makeup.

"I can't afford to be late."

"You know the breaks on the van are not great, so we need to take your truck," Renee said.

"We're going to have to start getting up earlier; I can't keep doing this." Dennis walked away.

"Fine, whatever!" Renee never took her eyes off of Jasmine.

* * *

At 10:17 AM church had started almost twenty minutes ago and Dennis was still in the car, at least six minutes away if he continued to do sixty-five to seventy miles per hour in a forty-five miles per hour zone.

"Slow down!" Renee yelled as she held onto the car handle.

"We're late as it is. I wouldn't be speeding if you weren't moving so slow," he shot back.

"I'm sorry. I was preparing breakfast for my family and getting the children ready for church." Renee rolled her eyes.

"All you got is excuses."

"Whatever, Dennis. I'm not going to argue with you."

Dennis's tires made a screeching sound as he turned the corner into the Gethsemane parking lot and weaved into the nearest parking spot. Dennis jumped out of the car and sprinted to the church. He ran up the steps and shot past the greeters and ushers. Eyes were focused on the front of the congregation, where his organ sat unmanned.

Right before Dennis sat down, Ron, the bass player, gave Dennis a look of playful disapproval for his tardiness. Dennis laughed and threw his hands up in surrender, pleased to have arrived at his faithful organ.

Dennis dug his fingers into the keys to enter the ensemble and moved his hands at a fever pitch pace along the ivory keys. As sweet as nectar, the music flowed through his veins and came out of his eyes.

When the song concluded, Dennis used the handkerchief from his pocket to wipe the sweat from his forehead and the back of his neck. "Praise Him!"

"Praise the lord, saints!" Timothy said from the pulpit.

Dennis looked at the nearly empty pews. Mere minutes ago, it had felt like the church was filled to capacity. Now he

saw how far and quickly Gethsemane had fallen from promi-
nence.

"Now, you have to keep in mind that Joshua was one of the
two that came back with a positive report. You have to have
the courage to go against the grain." Timothy received very
few "Amens."

It did not sit right in Dennis's stomach to see Timothy
stumble over metaphors and butcher a familiar passage in
the book of Joshua.

Members of the congregation walked in an assembly line
and formed a half-circle around the outside of the pulpit.
Their presence summoned various members throughout
the congregation to them for the altar call.

Very few people smiled. Most did not even lift their heads,
and instead they sleep-walked up to the altar. Renee stood
with her shoulders back and her hands folded. She watched
as Darius stood up and inched his way down the pew.

"God, I hope he doesn't come to me," Renee said to herself. His baggy clothes and thuggish demeanor were blatant
disrespect to God, and the fact that Timothy said nothing to
him about the way he dressed infuriated her even more.

Darius did not even make eye contact with Renee; he went
straight to Deacon Robinson. Renee sneaked a peek at her
husband, Dennis, on the organ. He wore the cream-colored
suit and orange tie she had bought him on Father's Day.

Renee got a whiff of strong perfume, turned around, and
saw Sister Thompson in a big, bright yellow business suit that
clinched to her voluptuous frame with a big yellow hat, decorated with plastic passion fruit.

"God bless you, Sister Thompson. How are you?" Renee
grabbed Sister Thompson by both hands.

"I'm blessed," Sister Thompson said.

"How may I pray for you?"

"Well, I got this really bad pain in my hip, and my doctor's appointment is tomorrow. I don't want to have to go to surgery."

"Well, we're going to pray for it right now in the name of Jesus." The women bowed their heads. Renee began to pray.

"Father, we ask right now that you heal my sister's body so that she will not have to go to surgery. Satan, we rebuke you in the name of Jesus. You are defeated, and God shall get the victory. In Jesus' name, amen."

"Amen." Sister Thompson lifted her head. "Thank you, Sister Childs. I love you." Sister Thompson gave Renee a hug.

As Sister Thompson walked back to her seat, Constance made her way to the altar. Their eyes locked, and Constance stepped uneasily toward Renee.

Haven't see her in a while, Renee thought to herself. "Good morning, Sister Anderson. How may I pray for you?"

"I need God to forgive me. I've made some really bad mistakes, and as a result, I haven't been coming to church lately. I just need to get my life together."

"Well, you know that God is able to do exceedingly and abundantly more than you can ever ask of Him."

Constance's hands were cold, and they trembled when Renee touched them.

"Father, we humbly come before you on behalf of my sister, Constance," Renee said after both women had bowed their heads. "Your Word declares that if we confess our sins, then you are faithful and just to forgive them. So we ask right now, Lord, that you forgive Constance of her sins and that you wash her and cleanse her of all unrighteousness. We ask right now in Jesus' name, amen."

Renee did not give Constance a hug. She just released her grip and handed Constance some tissue.

"Everyone give the Lord a hand clap," Timothy said from the pulpit.

Renee took her cue to sit down in the front row. She thought of a few possible scenarios behind Constance's journey to the altar. Maybe she had an issue with her album. Renee had recalled the couple of times that Constance had waited outside of Timothy's office after service to talk.

Renee got so caught up in her analysis of the situation that she tuned out and did not stand for the benediction. Dennis walked over to her from the pulpit.

"Honey!" Dennis said.

"Oh, I'm sorry, babe. I spaced out."

"You shouldn't do that in church. It's disrespectful." Dennis took a seat next to her.

"Okay, honey, I'm sorry. Don't talk to me like I'm some child." Renee grabbed her black leather purse and black coat and went to pick up Jasmine and Elijah from children's church.

Dennis returned to his organ and continued to play. Deacon Robinson, a tall man with salt and pepper hair, approached Dennis.

"Elder Childs?" Deacon Robinson said.

"Hey, Deacon Robinson, I heard you went fishing last week." Dennis shook Deacon Robinson's hand.

"Yeah, I went up to the lake and caught me a few. You need to come up with me sometime."

"No doubt, no doubt. So what's up?"

"I ain't going to beat around the bush. Members of the board are very unhappy with Timothy as pastor. We plan to have a meeting, and upon that meeting, I want to push for you to become pastor."

Dennis never took into consideration that the board members might be displeased with Timothy.

"I don't know what to say. You caught me off guard."

"Timothy is no more fit to be a pastor than I'm fit to be one of those rappers. The board voted him in because we trusted Ananias's wisdom and Timothy seemed like a good guy with enormous potential, but since he has taken over, the church has been going down, and we don't want to lose something that we've all worked so hard for"

"But Ananias—"

Deacon Robinson waved his hand to stop Dennis at mid-sentence. "Look, we love Ananias, but we have to come to grips with the fact that he is human, and maybe he didn't hear from God when he named Timothy as pastor."

"I don't know if that's the best thing to do. I mean, I would love to take over, but I'm sure you have better candidates."

"There are a few, but why go outside when we have a great candidate right here? You're an anointed man of God, a great husband, and a loving father. You can rebuild this ministry, and you know that you'll have a lot of people behind you."

Dennis pondered for a minute. "When's the meeting?"

"This Wednesday," Deacon Robinson said

"Let me pray about it. I'll call you tomorrow."

Dennis could not tolerate drama, so he avoided it at all cost. But in order to become senior pastor, it would be inevitable.

After she picked up Elijah and Jasmine from Sunday school, Renee felt a tap on her shoulder. Emerald stood in a sharp black business suit. Her shape reminded Renee of what her body used to look like before she had two kids.

"Hey, girl, that's a bad suit," Renee complimented.

"Thank you. You know I got to stay looking good. Listen, what are you doing this Saturday?" Emerald asked.

Renee rolled her eyes to the top of her head.

"Nothing off the top of my head, but I would have to double check. Why?"

"We haven't gotten together for coffee in a while. I was thinking that we could meet at Jazzy's on Saturday."

"Okay, well, call me this week to remind me."

"Will do. I'll see you later."

They waved at each other as Renee walked down the steps with a sleepy Jasmine in her arms as Elijah ran to the car. Dennis was already in the car. He turned the engine on as soon as Renee and Jasmine got down the steps.

He pulled out of the parking space and in front of the church.

Renee maneuvered Jasmine into the car seat while Elijah got in the driver's side. Renee then got into the truck and Dennis drove off. When they got a safe distance away, Renee leaned back in her seat.

"I think Timothy is cheating on Emerald."

CHAPTER SEVENTEEN

While the students in Timothy's English class finished their essays, Timothy worked on his sermon. There were a few whispers and occasional giggles, but overall, the class maintained order. Some students occasionally stared at the clock above the chalkboard.

Timothy opened his Bible to the book of Luke and the parable about the ten men with leprosy. Timothy centered his sermon on the premise that deliverance and blessings will come to you when you walk in faith.

"Quit looking at me, fag," Terrell yelled at Vernon.

Timothy looked as Terrell walked toward Vernon with both of his fists balled up.

"Sit down, Terrell," Timothy said.

Terrell did not acknowledge Timothy's command, and by the time he got to Vernon's desk, Terrell had hit him. The classroom exploded with "ooohs" and laughter.

"Quiet down, class. Finish your essays." Timothy created space between Vernon and Terrell. He grabbed Terrell by his shirt collar and slung him into a chair in the far right corner of the room. "You just earned a trip to the principal's office. Now sit there, and don't move."

Timothy turned around and saw Vernon with his head down. "Are you okay?"

Vernon did not respond. Timothy looked back at Terrell, who was running out of the classroom.

"Terrell, get back here!" Timothy called after him.

Timothy ran to the doorway to see Terrell sprinting toward the soccer field. Timothy did not run after him; instead, he went to the classroom phone behind the desk and dialed the principal's office.

"Principal's office," the secretary said.

"Hi, this is Mr. Wells in room nineteen. Terrell hit Vernon and ran out of the classroom toward the soccer field," Timothy said into the receiver.

"No problem. We'll get him and bring him back to class," the secretary said.

By the time Timothy hung up, the class was divided into the various cliques. Girls turned their tables toward each other and began to chatter, while the boys stood up and reenacted the altercation.

"Everybody back in your seats now!" Timothy yelled, but the bell for lunch sounded before the class could respond. The children stormed out of the classroom, but Vernon remained seated with tears in his eyes.

"Vernon, I'm sorry about what just happened." Timothy walked over to his student.

Vernon did not respond. He just sat at his desk and wiped the tears from his eyes. Timothy did not want to force the issue, so he made his way back to his desk and tried to finish his Bible study lesson.

"It don't matter. It's worse when I'm outside. They take me behind the bleachers and beat on me. They push me into the girls' bathrooms and call me all kinds of faggots and homos."

"Do you tell anyone?"

"I do, but all they say is that they didn't see them touch me and that I'm just trying to get attention."

Timothy took note that his once eager student had regressed to a quiet, timid young boy. Perhaps the constant taunts and fights with other students were the cause of Vernon's change in behavior.

"Listen, Vernon, the next time something happens, be sure to come tell me and I'll see to it that it never happens again. You shouldn't have to put up with that. You're a great student."

"Thank you, Mr. Wells." Vernon stood up and dragged his backpack out of the classroom.

Timothy doubted if any of his words had made a real impact on Vernon. He retrieved his Bible and glanced back at the passage in Luke and received a revelation. He knew that when the men with leprosy walked back, God healed them, but he now understood that when you walk in faith, God allows everything to fall into place.

The Bible had countless examples of men and women whose only qualification to accomplish the will of God was their faith, but like Vernon, Timothy allowed himself to be pushed around because of his lack of faith in his abilities to minister.

A rush of adrenaline sped through Timothy's body. It was a pivotal moment for him. Right in the middle of the classroom in the midst of torn papers and candy wrappers, Timothy knelt down on one knee and rested his hand on a nearby desk.

"God, I apologize for my attitude. I am not worthy of this blessing to minister to your people. But I am a willing vessel, and I'll do whatever you ask of me, and trust in the fact that you can do anything but fail."

Vernon counted every second of his lunch break. He went to the far corner of the soccer field and sat at a vacant bench. Little girls played jump rope, and boys maliciously jumped in to interrupt their game. The basketball courts were overcrowded with kids of both genders. Some kids even kicked a soccer ball around.

Vernon looked up to admire the baby blue sky with clouds like cotton balls, when a violent push caused him to crash onto the ground. His elbow scraped against the pavement.

"Don't sit on my bench, fag."

The sunlight blurred some of the attacker's facial features, but Vernon recognized the voice. It had to have been Manuel, because Vernon recognized Carlos and Sergio beside him; they followed Manuel like a shadow. Then Manuel haphazardly stepped out away from the sunlight to reveal his tall, football-player stature, and walked up to Vernon, who tried to get up.

"What, faggot?" Manuel kicked Vernon in the scrotum.

Vernon felt a sharp pain and numbness in his scrotum. He coughed to relieve the pain. He heard laughter and the sound of whistles, but no sound of an authority figure. Vernon turned to his side to further relieve the pain, only to absorb a kick in the stomach from Manuel. Carlos and Sergio joined in and kicked Vernon in the both the stomach and the mouth. Vernon's lips swelled up, and he could feel blood drip from his lip.

"You better quit looking at me in the locker room," Manuel said.

"Hey, what are you kids doing?" Mr. Jimenez, the sixth grade math teacher, asked. Manuel and his crew fled from the scene.

"Vernon, are you okay?" Mr. Jimenez helped Vernon up off the ground.

Vernon did not respond; instead, he tried to pick himself up off the ground. Mr. Jimenez, whose nickname was O.G. because he had tattoos on both arms, helped Vernon off of the ground and escorted him to the nurse's office. The relatively short distance from the playground to the nurse's of-fice seemed a mile away as Vernon's classmates watched him.

Mr. Johnson, the principal, caught up to the boys and made Manuel, Carlos, and Sergio stand up against the wall. Manuel had mouthed obscenities to Vernon before Mr. Johnson caught him.

They arrived outside of the nurse's office to find that three boys occupied the chairs next to the scale. One boy had an ice pack on his jaw; another boy was bent over with a trashcan in front of him, and the smell of vomit infected the air. The third boy just sat there with a mean look on his face.

"Wait here a minute." Mr. Jimenez went into the nurse's office. Vernon leaned against the wall, but he bent down to relieve some of the pain in his scrotum.

"What you in here for?" the mean-looking boy asked Vernon.

"I got into it with Manuel," Vernon replied

"You mean he mopped you up."

"Quiet, Benson!" the nurse said as she exited her office. "Come here, Vernon."

Vernon followed the nurse into her office as Mr. Jimenez left.

"Have a seat." The nurse pointed to the seat next to the door.

Vernon tried to sit down, but the pain caused him to squirm in his seat. The nurse went through the Rolodex while Vernon examined the poster of the endoskeleton and the countertop with a jar of cotton balls and Popsicle sticks.

"Is your mom at work right now?" the nurse asked him.

"I don't know." Vernon shrugged.

Vernon often confused his mother's work schedule with her social life. He heard his mother's voice then there was a beep, and he knew that the nurse had reached her voice-mail.

"Hi, this is Ms. Cooley. I'm the nurse at Beckett Middle

School. I have Vernon in the office right now, and he was in an altercation this afternoon. We're trying to contact a parent or guardian to come pick him up from school. Please give us a call. Thank you, bye." The nurse hung up the phone and examined the information card "This lists your uncle on here as a contact person."

Vernon's eyes enlarged. "He's not home right now."

"This lists a daytime number. Are you sure?"

"Yes, I'm sure. He's not home."

Before the nurse could reply, she heard a male voice outside her office.

"Now, sit over there, and do not put your head back." Timothy escorted a girl with a nose bleed to a nearby seat. As soon as the little girl sat down, Timothy walked into the nurse's office.

"Hello, Ms. Cooley. Karen took a dodge ball to the nose," Timothy informed the nurse.

"These kids need to find less violent ways to amuse themselves," the nurse said.

"Hello, Mr. Wells," Vernon said.

"What are you doing here?" Mr. Wells was surprised to see Vernon in the nurse's office.

"He got into a fight with Manuel," the nurse answered on Vernon's behalf. "I can't seem to get a hold of his mom."

"Can I please stay with you until the end of school?" Vernon asked Timothy.

"That's okay with me." Timothy turned his attention to Ms. Cooley.

"That's fine with me." Ms. Cooley shrugged her shoulders.

"I'll contact your fifth and sixth period teachers and have them send over your work."

Vernon's heart returned to normal. Timothy had saved him from his uncle . . . for now.

CHAPTER EIGHTEEN

Timothy sat and graded papers during lunch. On Fridays, he would try to have all of his papers graded so he could devote his weekends to church. This Sunday would mark five months since Timothy had taken over Gethsemane, and April first was less than a week away. Timothy knew he had to double his efforts for the church to survive the increase in rent.

He managed to get halfway through his third period's essays before Emerald walked in his classroom with a sandwich and a bottle of water in her hands.

"Hey, babe." Emerald placed the sandwich and water next to Timothy's Bible and gave him a kiss on the lips. "Long day?"

"Something like that." Timothy continued to grade papers.

"Listen, there's something I need to talk to you about." Emerald set her purse down on top of Timothy's desk.

"Okay, what is it?" Timothy asked.

"The board has called for an emergency meeting on Saturday morning."

"Saturday?"

"Yeah, I'm going to be honest with you. I think they're going to have you removed as pastor."

Timothy stood up and began to pace with his hands in his pocket. "I can't say that I'm shocked, but the way they're going about it is wrong."

"I know it is. I found out from another member."

"Everyone on that board was apprehensive about voting me in as pastor. I guess since the loss in membership, they have more than enough reason to remove me." Timothy rubbed his head.

"Don't sit there and feel sorry for yourself."

"Oh, I didn't say I was quitting. If they want me gone, then they're going to have to say it to my face." Timothy paced. "They better be prepared for a fight, because I'm not about to forfeit my destiny."

Emerald started to look around.

"What's wrong?" her husband asked.

"I'm on the lookout for my husband. Quick, kiss me before he comes back."

Timothy laughed and kissed Emerald. "What would I do without you?"

"I'm your helpmate. That's what I'm here for," Emerald said.

Retirement gave Ananias much time to improve his golf game. Ananias had a putting green in his backyard, but he felt like Tiger with Timothy standing beside him watching as he hit the ball. It rolled along the green and around the rim of the cup before it rolled out.

"I was making them before you showed up," Ananias grunted.

"Of course you were."

Timothy laughed and Ananias took another swing, and the ball went off the turf and into the grass.

"The devil is a liar."

"They're going to have a board meeting tomorrow to remove me as pastor," Timothy said directly.

"I'm not surprised." Ananias positioned himself to hit another ball. "Timothy, the board has gotten comfortable. They would rather play it safe than to step out on faith and risk potential disaster."

"I've finally accepted that this is the path that God has chosen for me, and now the board wants me gone?"

Ananias hit another ball that went into the hole. He then picked up the putter and rested it on his shoulder. "The enemy does not want you to discover your purpose, and now that you've discovered your purpose, the devil doesn't want you to fulfill it."

"Should I just go to the meeting and demand that they keep me as pastor?"

"I'm not saying that, but before this board meeting was even called, God had worked out the solution. So you can stand before the board without worry or fear."

"Are you ever going to come back to Gethsemane?"

"When the time is right." Ananias repositioned himself to take a swing. "Right now, I've been attending Bishop Watkins' church and helping him with a building campaign."

Jesus called the Pharisees a brood of vipers. Timothy considered the board members to be a brood of vipers. Of the nine, there were three with their proverbial finger on the pulse of the church. Deacon Robinson had served at Gethsemane for seventeen years, and he despised anyone born after the Reagan era. Deacon Simmons fit the ideal look of a deacon—middle-aged with little gray hair. He rarely performed any of the deacon's duties highlighted in the book of Timothy. Instead, he used charm to convince the masses otherwise. And then there was Sister Deborah, who was determined to give her opinion whether or not anyone asked for it.

Timothy stared at the three-headed beast and knew he had to take out at least one of them if he were to stand a chance.

"I thank you for allowing me attend your meeting. I just wanted to say that I appreciate all of your hard work over the last several months. It's been a difficult time with the ministry, but I am confident that we can get through this together." Timothy watched the board members look at each other disconcertedly.

"Look, Pastor, I never got a chance to say this, but I admire you for stepping up and trying to fill Ananias's shoes. It takes great courage to do what you did, and I applaud you for that," Deacon Robinson said.

"Thank you very much, Deacon Robinson," Timothy replied.

"With that said, however, I feel it's time that you hand the ministry over to a more experienced pastor."

"I agree," Sister Deborah concurred.

"I'm assuming that you have the perfect person in mind, don't you, Sister Deborah?" Timothy asked.

"I think that Elder Childs would be a better fit," Deacon Robinson offered.

"Ananias didn't seem to think so," Timothy said.

"And as much as I loved Ananias for thinking outside the box, it has not been a smooth transition. Let's just be honest here. The church is on dangerous ground, and unless we put the church in the hands of someone more capable, then we're going to be looking for a new building."

Timothy stood up and began to circle around the board members, and some of them avoided eye contact. "Did it ever occur to you that maybe the people who left were coming for the wrong reason? Ananias chose me to lead this ministry because he thought this ministry was stagnant. There were hardly any unfamiliar faces, and the vast majority of members were middle-aged. He chose me because I can reach the youth, and I'm not concerned with entertaining people."

Timothy stopped right behind Deacon Robinson. "I want to see people live the life that Jesus died for. I couldn't care less if that makes me popular or unpopular."

"And I respect and admire that, but youth can't pay the church's bills," Deacon Simmons said, much to the dismay of everyone in the room. "What? Let's be honest here. Teenagers ain't tithing!"

"When the finance department handed me the report last week, the adults don't tithe either. We need to be people of faith and trust that if we are faithful, then God will provide," Timothy replied.

"Maybe we can have a bake sale to raise money," Sister Deborah said.

"As much as I appreciate the idea and I know that it is rooted in the best of intentions, I have to say no to a bake sale. Sister Deborah, a bake sale will give us a hundred dollars at the most. We are better off asking everyone to give ten dollars," Timothy said.

"I just think that if we had someone with a strong anointing like Ananias, the church would be in better shape," Deacon Robinson said.

"When Ananias took over this ministry years ago, there were only fourteen members. The majority of them were members of his family. For years, the ministry struggled. Did you question whether or not Pastor Jones had a strong anointing?" Timothy asked.

Timothy's comment temporarily stopped Deacon Robinson in his tracks, but then he exploded. "I have served this ministry faithfully for nearly twenty years." He pointed at Timothy.

"We all have served this ministry faithfully, and we will continue to serve this ministry faithfully because we're not doing this for the approval of man, but for the approval of God," Timothy said to the dumbfounded board. He started to back away and head toward the door. "My apologies again for my intrusion, but unless you have heard from God, then I ask that you support me as your pastor and help me to find solutions to our problems." Timothy exited, closing the doors behind him.

CHAPTER NINETEEN

Constance beheld an enormous sanctuary that resembled an opera house with wall-to-wall carpet in royal blue. The balcony formed a U-shape high above the congregation. The floor of the auditorium consisted of three sections with dozens of rows of people. Two television cameras occupied the space between the front row and the stage. The cameras rotated from the audience to the stage.

Constance stood in the middle of the stage in a ruby dress with gold trimmings and microphone in hand.

"Praise the Lord, saints," Constance said.

"Praise the Lord," the audience said in an almost perfect cadence.

"I'm honored to be here to celebrate Bishop Mark's thirty-first anniversary." Constance turned toward Bishop Mark, who wore a navy blue suit with a head full of white hair and a ridiculously thick white mustache.

"I've been fortunate to hear Bishop Mark preach on many occasions, and whenever he asks me to sing, the only song I'm allowed to sing for him is 'His Eyes Are on the Sparrow.'"

So I know he won't let me off the stage until I sing this song, so you pray for me in Jesus' name."

Before a crowd of over nine thousand, Constance sang 'His Eyes Are on the Sparrow' with such fervor that everyone stood up in emotional euphoria. Faces were soaked in tears; saints shivered and waived their hands. Constance concluded the song and received a thunderous ovation.

She had barely gotten comfortable in her seat when James walked on the opposite end of the stage in a black T-shirt and jeans. He sat at the drum station. She could not seem to shake him no matter how much she avoided him.

The emcee for the event, a tall, sable-coated gentlemen in a black pinstripe suit that exposed his slim frame, returned to the stage.

"We are so blessed to have gospel recording artist Constance Anderson minister to us in song. Be on the lookout for her upcoming album." He signaled to the usher to bring forth a wooden case. The emcee then turned to Bishop Mark.

"Bishop, we would like to present you with this token of our appreciation for all your years of service."

Bishop Mark stood up and fixed his suit jacket. He then walked over to the emcee at a slow pace.

"Bishop, on behalf of all the members of New Covenant, we would like to present you with a brand new Mercedes Benz." After Bishop pretended to have a heart attack, he accepted the wooden case.

"God bless you and thank you." Bishop Mark handed the wooden box to his armor bearer, a short, stocky young man. "Now, don't go for no test drive," Bishop Mark said to him.

The congregation boomed with laughter. Bishop Mark managed a successful TV ministry, low-income apartment houses for some of his members, and a newly-built youth center. His success story inspired all pastors.

"Though I'm appreciative of the generous gift, nothing is

like preaching the gospel. Seeing Sister Anderson reminded me of what Pastor Jones and I used to do over there on Eighty-fifth and MacArthur Street. We'd take turns preaching the gospel to all the crack addicts, prostitutes, drug dealers, and gangsters. We were both scared, but when we got to preaching, the Holy Spirit moved, and folks started getting saved right then and there."

The congregation nodded in approval and shouted a few amens. Bishop Mark unbuttoned his jacket.

"Yeah, anybody that comes to me wanting to preach, I tell them to go to the street first, because if Jesus was alive today, that's where He'd be."

Constance slipped out the side door of the stage. On the other side of the door was a long hallway. The sound of Constance's heels echoed down the hallway.

"Constance?" James called as he closed the door.

"Listen, I have to go. I don't have time to talk." Constance stopped, but did not turn around.

"You don't return my phone calls." James's eyebrows gathered at the center of his forehead.

"I've been really busy lately, and I'm under a lot of stress with the album." Constance turned around and faced James.

"Wasn't it supposed to come out three weeks ago?"

"It was, but the label wasn't really feeling it, so Kevin and I went back and mixed a couple of songs, and he sent it back to the label."

"Look, ma, I got to ask you; are we together or what? Because I could be doing my own thing instead of waiting on you to decide when you have time for me."

"Now you see how it feels when someone doesn't have time for you." Constance put her hand on her hip.

"You know what? I'm tired of you talking about how I don't spend time with you. You didn't have a problem when you were in the studio all the time, so why are you now trying to flip the script on me?"

"Because I realize, James, you're not ready to grow and be a man. You're too busy trying to be a player. God only knows what you do when you're on the road."

James took a step back and waved his hands in disagreement. "Hold up, hold up! I ain't no player. You're the only girl I've been with," James said.

"And that was a mistake as well. We should've waited."

"Look, I know what the Bible says about marriage, but let's be real. It's darn near impossible to having feelings for someone and not express it. Besides, we've been careful."

Constance could recall several times when they did not use a condom, which was how she had gotten pregnant. She craved James, and though she always felt guilty after sex, she could not resist.

"So what? We're done now?" James said.

"We've been done, James; I was just too foolish not to see that."

James let out a nervous laugh and proceeded to scratch underneath his nose. "All right, cool then. You have a nice life."

"Whatever." Constance turned around and shoved open the double doors. When Constance got outside, her phone vibrated. She checked her cell phone. The front screen showed nine missed calls and three voicemails. She checked the call history and discovered that all of the missed calls came from Kevin.

"Why is he blowing me up?" she said to herself.

Constance speed dialed Kevin's cell phone, and by the second ring, he answered. "Hello?"

"Why are you blowing up my cell, knowing that I had to sing at Bishop Mark's church?"

"Are you done?"

"Yeah, I'm done."

"I need you to come to the studio as soon as possible."

"What's wrong?" Constance asked.

"I'll explain when you get here, but come now."

"All right." Constance hung up the phone. "This Negro must've lost his mind. This better be important."

Kevin sat at his desk with a somber look on his face. "They shelved the album."

"Why would they do that?" Constance said with a near hoarse voice.

"They weren't feeling it. They called me in today and told me that they want me to start working on Kiera's album."

"They can't do this! This is nine months of my life tied into this project. They can't just shelf it." Constance pounded her hand on the desk.

"I told you this was going to happen. I don't know what's going on between you and James, but you stopped writing and your songs sound like something is missing. I can't describe it, but it was like you couldn't get to that place that I needed you to be in. And look at you. You done picked up weight, ma."

"It has nothing to do with James. I've been under a lot of stress—so what if I picked up a little weight?"

"Well, whatever it was, you let it affect you bad. Now I don't know if they ever plan to release your album."

Constance paced the floor and bit her bottom lip. She stared at the zigzag patterns of the studio's carpet. Her mind was clouded with everything that had happened and how the one positive thing that meant most to her was now being taken away. Her eyes were as dry as a desert.

"I can't believe this is happening." Constance looked up to the ceiling. "God, you have to do something." She then sighed and turned to Kevin. "So what happens now?"

"I guess I'll call you when the label decides to pick up the project again."

"Am I going to get dropped from the label?"

"What do you want me to tell you, baby girl? This is the

age where people will download a CD in a heartbeat rather than pay for an album that only has four good songs on it. And the gospel music scene appeals to such a small market that you need to make sure your whole album is good. I go into a record store and polka music has a larger section than gospel music. This is the real world, and labels aren't going to pour money into an album that won't sell."

"This is all that I ever wanted to do!"

"You already know God got a strange timetable. It'll happen, Constance; it's just on God's timing."

"So what are you going to do now?" Constance asked.

"I got a few things in the works. I got Kiera's album, and I am even supposed to be doing something with Mary Mary, so I'll be okay. What about you?"

"I'm going to do something; I just don't know what." Constance rubbed her eyes.

Kevin stood up and walked around his desk to give Constance a big hug.

"Hang in there, ma. You're one of the best gospel artists I've ever worked with. You'll get there eventually."

"Thank you." Constance unclasped her arms and walked away.

A weight lifted from her shoulders with each step as she walked back to the elevator. The pressure of her album no longer existed. But that temporary relief soon turned into shame, because now everyone would wonder why her second album was never released, and people would entertain their own theories of what had happened, from a fight with the label over more money to no longer being anointed to sing.

Constance pressed the elevator button and stared at her reflection in the elevator door. It split in half once the doors opened.

CHAPTER TWENTY

Timothy found it difficult to talk to Darius from behind a thick sheet of glass. The smile that Timothy had grown accustomed to was gone. Instead, Darius's eyes were alarmed.

"Pastor, you got to help me," Darius said into the phone.

"What were you doing with a loaded gun?"

"I was going to get rid of it."

"You were going to?"

"I know I messed up, but I swear to you, I didn't do anything wrong. It's hard to break some habits when you're used to living a certain way."

"You're used to seeing the world from the perspective the enemy wants you to see it, but if you change your perspective, then you wouldn't need a gun to feel safe."

"I know. I got a little money stashed away, but not enough to spring me."

"The church is pretty tapped out, so I can't make any promises."

"I'm not asking for you to bail me out. I've been in here for a week and I'm due in court on Monday. I just want you to pray for me."

"What time is your hearing?"

"Nine o'clock."

"Spring break is this week, so I'm off. I'll be there."

"Good looking out." Darius's eyes started to wonder.

"Listen, Darius, I need you to focus and not let this situation get to you. You're not the first Christian to be put in jail before, but until I get you out, I need you to focus."

"But I'm saying, though, I became a Christian to keep from going to prison."

"Everything you have right now, you got by doing the devil's work. The devil is not going to let you become a Christian and walk around with his stuff. You're going to have to make a change and stop making excuses."

"A'ight, man." Darius looked away.

"Stay strong." Timothy hung up the phone and left the county jail with a tension headache that only increased as he walked back to his car.

A whole day passed. Darius occupied a seat in the TV lounge. He rubbed his hands against his jeans nervously. No one really bothered him. Most of the guys watched sports. A Mexican guy with a bald head and tattoos that flowed from his neck down to his forearm stared at Darius from the other side of the court. Like Darius, the Mexican appeared to have distanced himself from his ethnic group.

Since becoming a Christian, Darius had taken on a more passive approach, until the guy got up and made his way toward him. Darius stood up with both of his fists balled up. It was foolish to think that he would sit in jail for a week without being tested.

"It's cool, fool. No beef," the Mexican said.

Darius retreated back to his bench and sat down. The Mexican took a seat next to Darius and removed from his front pocket an almost empty pack of cigarettes and offered it to Darius.

"Naw, I'm good." Darius held up his hand to refuse the offer.

"What they get you for?" The Mexican put a cigarette to his lips and lit it. He then pulled the cigarette away from his lips and blew out a long smoke that faded in the air.

"Old nature."

"What?" the Mexican asked.

"Nothing, I got out the dope game, but there are still some old habits I couldn't shake and they got me caught up. What about you?"

"I went for a ride in someone else's car," the Mexican answered.

The two laughed like two guys on the corner.

"My mans used to boost cars, then one day this shorty he used to mess with, her dude shot him up just after he lifted a Honda," Darius said.

"For real? Dang! The game ain't no joke."

"Tell me about it. It almost took my life twice."

"Yeah, I've been shot too." The Mexican pointed to the scar on his shoulder "Yeah, I was raised Catholic and I believe in God and all, but I don't think He knows what's going on."

"He does. It's us that got it twisted. The devil is straight on the grind trying to bring us down."

"I got to feed my family, though."

"I feel you, but you have to ask yourself, how are you feeding your family if you're in here?"

The Mexican did not give a quick response, and Darius knew he was giving his words some thought.

"That's real talk," the Mexican said.

"I decided to get my life together. I might be foolish, but I believe that I still have a chance at a good life. I believe Jesus can show me the way."

"Darius White!" the guard yelled from the other side of the yard.

"What's up?" Darius made eye contact and gave a head nod.

"You got a visitor."

That must have meant that Pastor Wells came back to visit. Darius got up and walked toward the guard.

"Hey!" the Mexican yelled.

Darius stopped and turned around.

"What church you go to?"

"Gethsemane!"

"I'll have to check you out when I get out. My name is Roberto."

"Darius, man. That's what's up."

Darius smiled. The speech Timothy had given him about a divine destiny echoed in his head.

Judge Powell had sentenced three men to jail before Darius's case was called. Darius could only hope that he did not have a good memory.

"Mr. White, I distinctly remember telling you that if I ever saw you in my courtroom again, I would put you away. Am I right?"

"Yes, Your Honor," Darius said.

Judge Powell took off his glasses and pointed at Darius. "So, Mr. White, please tell me why not even six months has passed and you're back in my courtroom again. Did you think I was playing with you?"

"No, Your Honor. I got out and I turned my life around. I started going to church, and I even started to look for a job."

"Mr. White, I'm not impressed when someone tells me that they go to church. My mother used to tell me that even the devil goes to church." He scanned Darius's record. "When I have a case that involves a concealed weapon in the possession of a convicted felon, well, that is more than enough reason for me to give you time and go on with my day."

Darius knew that the judge was not going to yield just because he became a Christian. Even Darius himself found it difficult to believe that he had made a 180-degree turn. But in the midst of an inevitable sentence, Darius felt complete peace. The last six months had been a dog fight, but Darius stood convinced that even now, God was still with him.

"Do you have anything to say for yourself?" Judge Powell asked.

"Your Honor I can't justify my actions. What I did was stupid, and there's no excuse. But I have turned my life around and my faith lies in God. I'm not even supposed to be alive, yo, for real! But God has kept me around for a reason, and if that reason is for me go to prison and witness to my brothers on lockdown, then I'll go."

"Your Honor, may I say a few words?" Timothy stood up and walked toward Darius.

"Are you his legal counsel?" Judge Powell asked.

"No, I'm Pastor Timothy Wells, senior pastor of Gethsemane Community Church. I took over Gethsemane after Pastor Ananias Jones retired."

"Pastor Wells, I would not be inclined to mention Pastor Jones's name in this courtroom seeing that he is a terrible golfer and an even worse poker player."

The handful of people in the courtroom laughed.

"While all that may be true, what is also true is that Darius is a changed man. He's come a long way since the last time you've seen him, and it would be a shame to send a young man with enormous potential to prison. I have plans to put Darius over our evangelism ministry, where I think his testimony will help keep some of our youth off the streets and out of your courtroom."

"You must have a lot of faith in this young man," Judge Powell said.

"Yes, Your Honor, I do."

"Do you see that this man is putting a lot of faith in you?" Judge Powell asked Darius.

"Yes, Your Honor?" Darius said with a smirk.

Judge Powell put his glasses back on and scanned over Darius's file. "I am a man of my word, Mr. White, and though I appreciate Pastor Wells's comments, I can not afford to let you off the hook. I sentence you to one year in the county jail. You have until April thirty-first to report to the Santa Clara County Jail." Judge Powell banged on his gavel. All of Darius's dirty deeds had finally caught up with him, but a year was doable.

"I'm so sorry, Darius," Timothy said.

"Don't even worry about that, but just so you know, when I get out, I'm bringing some new members with me."

"Bring them on." Timothy shook Darius's hand. "You stay strong."

Darius knew that with the strength of Christ Jesus, he would.

CHAPTER TWENTY-ONE

Dennis had fallen behind on his workload and needed to work overtime, but the more employees that left, the more Dennis's flesh craved Cecilia. Both excitement and dread lacerated him.

You're okay, so long as you don't initiate any contact. Just stay at your desk and finish up. You'll leave after she leaves.

Dennis tried to refocus his attention on work, but thoughts of Cecilia in her short miniskirt imploded in his brain. Renee left two messages that Dennis did not bother to return. Renee nagged too much for Dennis to be bothered with her.

"You want the rest of this, papi?" Cecilia held out a half-eaten burrito.

"No, thank you, I'm full." Dennis rubbed his stomach.

Cecilia walked over and set the burrito on Dennis's desk. His body weakened the closer she got to him. His mind was susceptible to all kinds of fantasies of Cecilia naked and her body spread out across his desk.

"You need to go home," Dennis suggested

"I don't have nothing waiting for me at home but a lazy cat."

"Where's Miguel?"

"He's with his father this week. Thank God. It gives me a break."

Aroused by the sight of Cecilia, Dennis could not move away from his desk. He even ignored the phone when it rang three times.

"Your wife's calling." Cecilia pointed her head toward the caller ID on the phone.

"I'll call her back in a minute; I need to get this done." Dennis stacked piles of papers together.

Cecilia began to massage Dennis's shoulders until the tense muscles in his shoulders loosened. "Relax. You're too tense," she cooed to him.

"I have a lot on my plate."

She continued to work her hands up toward his neck and back down his shoulders before she stopped at his chest.

"That'll be a hundred dollars," Cecilia said as she patted Dennis's chest.

Dennis got up and faced Cecilia. "Thank you so much for all your hard work. My wife was nervous about me starting my own business, but you have been the heart and soul of Childs Construction."

"Thank you for giving me a job despite the fact that I had very little experience."

The top of Cecilia's head nestled under Dennis's chest and her arms firmly locked around his waist. Without exaggeration, Cecilia's hair smelled like roses, and it tempted him to kiss her on the top of her head. Cecilia looked up and cuddled her lips with Dennis's bottom lip.

Dennis tried to inhale every single drop of flavor from Cecilia's lips. His veins were on fire. Dennis pushed aside the papers on his desk, and Cecilia sat on the edge of it. Dennis caressed every part of her body, only intensifying his desire to have her.

Dennis watched Cecilia sensually unbutton her blouse.

"Oh my God, what am I doing?" Dennis asked.

He stopped Cecilia before she took off her blouse and he turned away. Dennis kept his back turned to her. He did not have the courage to face her; instead, he hoped that she would be overcome with shame and flee his office, which she did. He caught a glimpse of Cecilia from his peripheral vision as she left his office. Moments later, her car door slammed and her car pulled away.

It only took five minutes for Dennis to break an eleven-year covenant of marriage. The action was so sudden and miniscule that Dennis stood in disbelief over what had transpired in his office.

"It's okay. You didn't cheat. You didn't go all the way. You stopped before things went further," he said out loud as he paced nervously.

The phone rang and Dennis felt his heart stop. He looked on the caller ID and saw that it was Renee.

Dennis figured he had to answer; otherwise she would suspect something was going on. "Hey, babe!"

"The kids and I have been waiting for you to get home."

"I'm sorry. I had a few things to finish up, and I'll be home in a few minutes," Dennis said.

"Drive safely. I love you."

"Okay, bye." Dennis hung up the phone and rubbed his face. "Lord, please forgive me." He stared at his wedding band.

Jasmine giggled from Dennis's bear hug. He smothered her dimpled face with kisses.

"It is way past her bedtime," Renee said as she put the dishes away.

"Tuck me in, tuck me in!" Jasmine giggled and pleaded with her father.

"Okay, honey." Dennis allowed Jasmine to lead him by the

hand into the bedroom she shared with her brother. Elijah sat on his bed playing video games.

"Time for bed, champ," Dennis said to Elijah, who then turned off the video game without any resistance.

The two kids got in the bed, and Dennis stood between the two beds and helped tuck Jasmine in. He then got down on one knee.

"Oh gracious and heavenly Father, we ask that you watch over Elijah and Jasmine as they sleep and that you bless them to have a good day tomorrow and that they listen to their teachers and parents. We thank you for all that you have blessed me with in Jesus' name, amen."

"And God bless my mom and dad," Elijah added.

"Amen," Jasmine said.

A tear came to Dennis's eyes, but the darkness concealed his humanity. For years, he acted as though his children were a burden, but tonight he was reminded how precious they were and how much they loved him despite his actions.

"Goodnight, sleep tight." Dennis turned on Jasmine's night light and closed the door behind him.

As Dennis walked into the kitchen, Renee had loaded the last dish in the dishwasher and wiped off the grease from the stove. "You were extremely affectionate tonight," she said to him.

"I didn't notice."

"I did. I missed the loving side of you. You've been so stressed out with work and church, and I know that I only add to it."

"You could save the sarcasm." Dennis sat down at the dinner table.

"I'm serious; you really are a great husband. That's why I get so mad when I feel like someone is taking advantage of you."

"Timothy is actually doing a pretty good job considering the circumstances."

"Please! At the rate we're going, we're going to be back at a storefront."

"Don't say that."

"We wouldn't have lost so many members if you were pastor. Karen told me that James left and went to New Covenant. He grew up playing the drums at Gethsemane. He's an anointed drummer, now he's gone."

"You know what, baby? I'm really tired and I don't feel like talking about church or ministry."

"I'm sorry, baby." Renee walked over and gave Dennis a big hug and a kiss on the cheek. "I'm terrible for constantly bombarding you with this issue."

"It's okay. I'm going to take a shower and get some sleep." Dennis pulled away from Renee.

Satan robbed Dennis of his precious moment. *How could you break her covenant? She would be devastated; the kids would be hurt too.*

The next day at work, Dennis developed a cramp in his neck. It was 11:22 AM, and there was no sign of Cecilia. His focus shifted from his work to the window of his parking lot.

Where could she be? I hope she didn't quit. She might be meeting with Renee now to tell her. I should've gone all the way. At least then I would have a good reason for feeling guilty.

Chris, a young man with a surfer look, walked by and caught Dennis's attention.

"Chris," Dennis yelled.

"Yes, boss?"

"Have you seen Cecilia?"

"No, I haven't. I think she called in. Do you need anything?"

"No, I'm fine." Dennis put a stack of papers in a neat pile.

"Okay then." Chris walked away.

"Satan, I rebuke thee in the name of Jesus. You'll not cause me to feel condemned in any way. You're defeated, and you're a liar. The truth is not within you."

Part of Dennis did not want Cecilia to show up. He did not want to confront his infidelity. But even still, Dennis drew pleasure from guesswork of what Cecilia might wear today.

He let an idea get into his head that Cecilia might have sent him an e-mail in which she poured out her emotions to him. He went to pull up his work e-mail and accelerated past all the porn sites and deleted them one by one before he accessed his e-mail, only to find that in the seventeen unread messages, not one of them was from Cecilia. Then suddenly, he heard a knock on the door.

"It could be her," he said under his breath. "Come in!"

"Good morning, sir." Timothy entered Dennis's office.

"What a pleasant surprise."

"Well, the kids are out on spring break, and usually we play phone tag, but this is too important to leave on your voicemail," Timothy said.

"What's going on?"

"I was wondering if you could preach on Sunday."

"Yeah! Of course, I would love to, praise God." Dennis's nervousness turned into excitement.

"You deserve to bless the congregation with a word."

"Okay, well, I will definitely do that."

"And you're preaching the main service," Timothy said with a smile.

"Well, I thank you for giving me an opportunity to preach."

"I didn't know what you were doing right now, but I figured we could go to breakfast, and I can share with you some ideas I have about the ministry. I would love to get your insight."

"I would love to, but I don't plan to go to lunch for another hour or so." Dennis looked at his watch.

"No problem."

There was another knock on the door.

"Come in!" Dennis called out.

Cecilia walked in with no makeup and her hair pulled

back into a ponytail. "I didn't mean to interrupt you," she said.

"Oh no, this is my pastor—Timothy Wells." Dennis did not know if it was God or the devil who arranged these events; he only hoped that Cecilia would not make a scene and expose his infidelity.

"Pleasure to meet you." Timothy shook her hand.

"Likewise," Cecilia said.

"Cecilia is a great administrative assistant," Dennis complimented.

Dennis noticed that Timothy paid close attention to his interactions. It was important for him to relax and not arouse suspicion.

"Listen, Dennis, I'll catch up with you later." Timothy gave Dennis a pat on the shoulder.

"Okay, Pastor."

"It was nice meeting you again," Timothy said to Cecilia before he exited the office.

"He's really young to be a pastor," Cecilia said.

"Tell me about it."

Dennis noticed the acne on Cecilia's face; her hair did not smell like roses, and the long gray T-shirt and denim jeans hid her hourglass frame.

"Cecilia, last night was a mistake. I'm sorry I crossed the line, and I don't want you to quit," Dennis told her.

"Last night was a mistake, but I'm not sorry, and that's why I will quit."

"I'm married; I should've been the responsible one. I love my wife very much."

"You love her, but you're not in love with her, and you're not happy in your marriage."

"You don't know that." Dennis's eyebrows nearly touched the center of his forehead at Cecilia's outlandish claim.

"Carlos left me because he was bored. He left my son and me for another woman who knew how to spice things up. I

blame myself, because when I look back, all I ever did was complain."

Dennis never considered the idea that he was unhappy in his marriage. Between pockets of marital bliss and extreme arguments, there existed a vast mundaneness. Only now, as he stared at this vixen, did he realize something was inherently wrong in his marriage.

"So what happens now?" Dennis asked

"I don't need any drama in my life, and it's on you whether or not to tell your wife. I just want my final check so I can leave."

Cecilia offended Dennis's ego by her willingness to end the affair so easily. Only three people knew about last night: God, Dennis, and Cecilia. He found comfort in the fact that Cecilia did not want to ruin his marriage, but how could he reconcile things with God without a confession to Renee?

Every Saturday night, Dennis would always sit in his home office and work on a sermon. He knew that come Sunday his designated place was behind the organ, but it felt good anyway.

This night, Dennis thumbed through his previously written sermons in search of the right one to deliver. He combed through the archives, but could not find a single sermon his spirit connected with. Instead, his mind deviated to thoughts of Cecilia and how sweet her lips tasted. How could the Latin seductress have had such an average appearance the other day?

By midnight, Dennis had gone through his entire catalog of sermons and none of them sufficed. He decided to rehearse the songs for Sunday's praise and worship, in an effort to take his mind off of his sermon. With heavy eyes and a body that shook from a massive caffeine intake, Dennis decided to use a tried and true sermon. He turned his Bible to Acts 16:25. "And at Midnight." The phrase sparked Dennis's

imagination. A familiar passage known to stir up crowds. Dennis had preached a sermon on this passage to a church in Salinas. He remembered that the message was well received.

Ananias rarely let anyone preach. Dennis felt that Ananias had held him back, but he never wanted to voice his opinion.

Renee entered the room with a bag of sunflower seeds and iced tea. When Dennis turned around, his whole countenance changed.

"Is everything okay, baby?" Dennis asked

"I thought you would want a snack." Renee set the bag of sunflower seeds and iced tea on his computer desk.

"Thanks, babe." Dennis threw a handful of sunflower seeds into his mouth.

"How's it coming along?"

"Good." Dennis spit some of the seeds out on a napkin. "I wrote this sermon over two years ago; I'm just going to polish it up for tomorrow."

Renee wrapped her arms around Dennis's neck and gave him a kiss on the side of the head.

"What's that for?" Dennis rubbed her forearm.

"I'm so proud to be your wife. I know sometimes I can be a little bossy, but I want you to know that I love you very much and you're going to do great tomorrow."

"I haven't been as good of a husband as I should've been."

"I'm lucky to have you," Renee said as she gave him a kiss.

She left the room. He could not tell Renee about the affair. He did not want to break her heart.

On Sunday, the congregation stood on their feet the entire time Dennis led praise and worship. He plunged his fingers into the keys until his fingers started to blister.

The new drummer was a young man named Quincy, who was a student at De Anza College. Fred had played bass gui-

tar for years, and of course, there were several members who
had brought their own tambourines. Dennis's adrenaline
built up to anticipation for this moment.

"Praise the Lord, saints," Timothy said.

"Praise the Lord," the congregation replied

"Whew, let's give another hand clap to our musicians for
the wonderful job they're doing."

The congregation gave a generous ovation.

"Today we are honored to be blessed by our very own associate Pastor, Dennis Childs, who is going to deliver the
message for today. Please stand and receive the spokesperson
for the King of Glory, Pastor Dennis Childs."

The congregation gave him a thunderous ovation. Renee
stood in the front pew and held Jasmine's hand as Elijah
leaned against Renee. Dennis approached the pulpit, and
Timothy handed him the microphone.

"Bring it!" Timothy said.

"Thank you." Dennis set his Bible down and looked out
among the sanctuary and observed a half-full congregation.
"Praise the Lord, saints."

"Praise the Lord," they replied.

"Give an honor to our pastor, Pastor Wells, First Lady, and
my wife, Renee, who I love dearly. The scripture for today's
message can be found in the Book of Acts 16:25. A familiar
passage," Dennis said as he put on his reading glasses.

"And at midnight, Paul and Salas were praying suddenly.
There was such a violent earthquake that the foundations of
the prison were shaken. And the church said Amen."

"Amen," the congregation said.

"Oh, gracious and heavenly Father, we ask right now that
you open our hearts and minds. Speak through your servant
today."

As Dennis began to pray, an image of Cecilia on his desk,
unbuttoning her blouse, popped into his head.

"In Jesus' name, I pray. Amen" Dennis took off his glasses.

"It's important that no matter what situation you're in, you have to remember to give God the praise."

Satan managed to sneak his way into Dennis's thoughts.

You're a hypocrite. You don't have any business up here preaching.

Renee gave Dennis an awkward look as he stumbled through his introduction.

"When you find yourself in a stressful work environment and there are threats of layoffs, you need to praise God until the foundations of your work environment are shaken."

Dennis managed to garner a handful of "Amens," but when he glanced down at his sermon notes, he realized that he had just skipped points one and two.

"Paul and Salas were in the foulest part of the prison according to church history, and yet they gave God the praise."

Dennis received fewer "Amens" and more blank stares.

They're not going to listen to an adulterer, Satan reminded him.

The clock in the back of the sanctuary above the sound room turned to 12:11 PM. Altar call started at 12:30, and yet within eleven minutes, Dennis had touched on every topic of his sermon without one fully developed point and none of his subpoints. Dennis took a sip of water from the stand next to the pulpit in order to buy time.

"I don't know about you, but many times I find myself needing to praise God until the foundations are shaken, until you're delivered, until your marriage is restored, until you're debt free."

Quincy moved over from the drum station to the organ, and for every point Dennis emphasized, Quincy thronged on a high key.

"Whew, you got to praise him until the foundation shakes. Touch your neighbor and say, 'Neighbor . . .'"

"Neighbor!" the congregation said.

"You got to praise Him until it falls off."

"You got to praise Him until it falls off."

"Now give three people a high-five."

The bulk of the congregation got up and gave each other a high-five.

Go ahead and keep the front going, Satan taunted.

The musicians continued to play. The congregation continued to dance and shout. Dennis stood next to the pulpit in tears. He figured the congregation would assume that the Holy Spirit had moved him

CHAPTER TWENTY-TWO

For Vernon, it was another weekend at his uncle's while his mom went out. It came too soon and lasted too long. He had held Autumn captive all Saturday morning and afternoon, and played all the games she wanted to play regardless of how stupid they seemed. He refused to let her go to sleep. Every time Autumn tried, Vernon would tickle her until she would jump up and ran out of the living room. It bought him more time.

Uncle Alex entered the living room, where his niece and nephew played while he baby-sat them.

"Vernon, come look at this model car. I got a Chevy Impala," his uncle said from the kitchen.

"No thank you, Uncle Alex," Vernon replied.

"Come on in the back. Stop playing with them girl toys. That's why those kids talk about you now."

"God, please protect me and my sister from our uncle," Vernon softly prayed as his nerves began to rustle.

For now, the company of his sister protected Vernon, but it was short-lived.

"I'm tired, Vernon." Autumn yawned.

"When we're at home, you won't even allow me to do my homework; now you want to complain," Vernon snapped.

"Let her go to sleep. It's time for her nap anyways." Alex took Autumn by the hand and led her away into the room next door to the living room.

"God, please protect me. Please, God. I won't misbehave or anything. Please don't let him touch me."

Just in case God did not answer his prayers, Vernon scanned the room for a weapon in the midst of model cars, collector's toys, video games, and DVDs.

On the coffee table, a black pen without its cap sat on top of a magazine. Vernon rushed over to the coffee table and slid the pen into his pocket. The door closed and he could hear the heavy feet of his uncle coming back into the room. Vernon devised an improbable plan.

If he could subdue his uncle long enough to grab Autumn and run out the door, then they might have a chance to make it up the hill to Mr. Claiborne's house, which was at least five houses away.

"What have you been telling your mom?" Alex walked toward Vernon.

"Nothing, I ain't told my mom nothing!" Vernon backed up until the wall stopped him.

Alex confined Vernon to a corner next to his trophy case and poked Vernon in the chest. "If you told your mother anything, I will kill you. You understand me?"

"Yes!" Vernon said while he rubbed his chest.

"Take off your shirt!"

"No!" Vernon screamed with tears in his eyes.

"Stop crying." Alex grabbed Vernon by the throat and smacked him across the face. "Take your shirt off now!"

Alex released his grip and Vernon started to take off his T-shirt. Alex's eyes enlarged and a sinister smile emerged as he viewed Vernon's frail body. Vernon could not understand what it was about his body that aroused his uncle. He hated his body, and the kids at school always teased him about it.

"Now take off your pants," Alex ordered.

Vernon began to unbuckle his belt. The smile on Alex's face widened, and Vernon no longer viewed his uncle as human, but as a monster. His eyes turned red like fire and his teeth turned into fangs. Vernon unzipped his pants, and Alex moved in closer and squeezed Vernon's face until his lips poked out and a snot bubble came out of his nose. Vernon put up a futile attempt to prevent his uncle from kissing him, but it didn't work.

Filled with rage and hatred, Vernon reached in his pocket, grabbed the pen, and began to stab his uncle blindly.

Blinded by his uncle's girth, Vernon jabbed until he felt a sticky fluid that he knew was his uncle's blood. Alex's knees buckled and he fell like a giraffe onto the PlayStation set. Alex lay on the floor with his blue denim jeans soaked in blood and his eyes transfixed on the blood on his hands, while Vernon stood over him, victorious.

Vernon ran to the room next door and slammed his body into the door as he opened it. Autumn jumped up in a panic at the sight of Vernon.

"Oh my God, you're bleeding," Autumn screamed.

"It's okay. It's not my blood, but we have to go right now, Autumn," Vernon said after a quick examination.

He yanked Autumn by the arm and dragged her like a load of laundry out of the room. Vernon got one foot out of the front door before his uncle grabbed his shoulders.

"You little bastard," Alex said in weakened state.

"Run, Autumn," Vernon screamed to Autumn, and she obeyed her brother's request.

Alex swung Vernon around. No longer did Vernon see his uncle as a monster, but as a weak, scared individual. Vernon proceeded to stab his uncle in the forearm with the pen he still held in his hand, until Alex released his grip.

Vernon sensed freedom and ran out the front door. Just when he made it outside of the house, a car came to a screeching halt and collided with Autumn. Vernon watched as his baby sister flew off of the ground and bounced onto the concrete.

"Oh my God!" He screamed as he rushed toward the body. He picked her up, and she lay unconscious in his arms.

Timothy and Emerald ate dinner and laughed without a care in the world.

"Babe, you should've seen the look on this kid's face when I caught him tagging yesterday. The boy looked like he saw Jesus." Timothy scraped the leftover food into the wastebasket and placed his dish into the sink.

"Oh, no, put it in the dishwasher." Emerald pointed at Timothy's dish.

"It's a shame you have to pry a spray can out of a nine-year-old's hand." Timothy spun Emerald around and wrapped his arms around her waist. He kissed her on the neck and small goose bumps appeared.

"I'm proud of you for standing up and fighting," she said with her eyes closed, taking in the after-effect of her husband's kiss.

Emerald turned around and wrapped her arms around Timothy's neck. "Baby, I keep telling you that God will work it out. You just got to do your part and preach the gospel." Emerald stole a kiss from Timothy.

Before he got a chance to respond, the phone rang. Timothy did not break away from the kiss until the second ring. He glanced at his cell phone. The caller ID showed a phone number from the County Hospital.

"Let it ring." Emerald kissed Timothy on the neck.

"It's from the hospital." Timothy broke away from Emerald's grip and answered the phone. On the other end was a frantic voice he could not make out.

"Mr. Wells! Mr. Wells!"

"Who is this?"

"It's Vernon, Mr. Wells. I need you to come to the hospital quick. A car hit my sister, and she's in critical condition."

"Oh my God. You're at County General?"

"Yes!"

"Okay, I'll be there in a minute. Just calm down, okay?" Timothy said and then hung up the phone.

Timothy recognized the anxiety on Emerald's face.

"That was one of my students, Vernon. A car hit his sister."

"Oh my God, is she all right?"

"Vernon says her condition is critical. He wants me to come down there."

"Where's his parents?"

"The father died years ago, and I presume the mother must be at the hospital now and he just wants me there to pray for them. I won't be long."

"So you're going over there?"

"I have to!"

"Okay, fine. Be safe," Emerald said.

"I'll come back as soon as possible."

"That's fine."

Timothy owed Emerald a lot of romantic nights, and just when he thought that he could begin to repay them, he got called away.

County Hospital reeked of vomit and latex gloves. Timothy wove his way through the sick babies, the old man in the wheelchair with a violent cough, and the elderly lady who pushed around her oxygen tank. He passed the overhead television that displayed the *Tonight Show* and made his way through the double doors.

He followed the signs that led him to the intensive care unit and found Vernon at the end of the hall, frozen like a statue.

"Vernon," Timothy called to him.

Vernon turned to Timothy, but did not move. When Timothy got close enough, Vernon gave him a firm hug.

"It's all my fault," Vernon cried.

There were too many unanswered questions. Through the doorway there lay a beautiful little girl in a deep sleep with tubes in her mouth and an IV catheter in her arm.

"Are you the father?" a heavy-set Caucasian police officer asked.

"No, I'm his teacher. What happened?"

"We're still trying to work out the details, but it would appear that in an effort to escape their uncle, Autumn Bailey ran out into the street and was hit by a car."

"Why was she running from your uncle?" Timothy asked Vernon, who only returned a cold stare.

"When we arrived at the scene, Mr. Hendricks had been stabbed several times in the leg, lower abdomen, and forearm with a pen. This young man admitted that he stabbed him in self-defense. We also discovered that Mr. Hendricks had several adult materials with underage minors in them. We arrested him on suspicion of child pornography and child molestation."

Timothy looked at Vernon in disbelief. This same boy who refused to fight the classroom bully had defended himself against a grown man.

"Where's his mother?" Timothy asked.

"We've left several messages, no response."

"Could you please pray for her, Mr. Wells?" Vernon asked in a cracked voice

"Of course I will. You pray with me, okay?" Timothy replied.

"God doesn't want to hear me. He's punishing me."

Timothy pulled Vernon away from him and placed his hands firmly on his shoulders. "No, He's not; He loves you and your sister!"

"Then why is this happening to me?"

"I don't know why, but what I do know is God still has the final word. Your sister can come out of this, but you need to believe—okay?" Timothy said to Vernon, who could only muster a head nod. "We're going to do this together, okay?"

"All right," Vernon agreed.

Timothy and Vernon slipped into Autumn's room. Timothy took a moment to listen to the sound of an oxygen tank and the occasional beeps of a monitor. He gently placed his hands over Autumn's chest, and Vernon followed suit and placed his hands on her feet.

"Father, in the name of Jesus, we ask right now that you do not let the enemy steal this beautiful, precious life," Timothy said before Vernon's sweet, sincere prayer interrupted his train of thought.

"Lord, please save my sister. I promise I'll go to church and not fall asleep. I promise to play with her whenever she wants. Please, God, please. I need her!"

"Lord, don't let this little boy experience something so devastating. Lord, the doctors have gone as far as they can go. Now is the time for you to come in and bring forth a miracle. We ask right now in Jesus' name, that you restore her in perfect health; no broken bones. That her survival will be a testament of your awesomeness. In Jesus' name, amen."

Vernon hugged Timothy at the conclusion of the prayer.

"I'll stay with you until you mother comes," Timothy said

"Thank you,' Mr. Wells."

At the break of day, Timothy was asleep in the chair next to the police officer. Vernon still stood frozen like a statue. He watched Autumn until Kristal finally arrived and ran down the hallway.

"Oh my God, my baby!" Her scream awakened Timothy and got the attention of the on-duty police officer. Kristal grabbed Vernon by his shirt and swung him around.

"What happened? What did you do?"

"I didn't do nothing." Vernon tried to fight away from his mother.

"Don't lie to me! You were probably playing too much and she ran out in the street to get away from you."

"It wasn't Vernon's fault," Timothy interjected

"What are you doing here?" Kristal snapped at Timothy.

"Vernon called me when he couldn't get a hold of you."

"Ma'am, I'm Detective Sanders, and we arrived on the scene to find that your son, in self-defense, stabbed his uncle, Mr. Alex Hendricks," the detective told her.

"What happened?"

"It would appear that Mr. Hendricks tried to molest your son. He also featured your son in video material."

Her eyes scanned each individual in search of clarity.

"Ma'am, I have to ask this: Were you aware of any strange behavior with your brother?"

"No, of course not! I wouldn't have left him with my kids if I were." Kristal pulled Vernon in close and rubbed his head.

"Well, I'm glad you're here now," Timothy told Kristal. "I'm going to head home. If you need anything, don't hesitate to call." Timothy patted Vernon on the shoulders.

"Thank you, Mr. Wells," Vernon said as he held onto his mother.

"I appreciate you for taking care of my son until I arrived," Kristal thanked Timothy.

"That's my reasonable service." He smiled.

"Ma'am," the detective interrupted, "when you have a minute, I would like to ask you a few questions."

"Sure." Kristal sobbed.

It was not too long after Timothy left that Autumn blinked. Later, she opened her eyes, and by mid-afternoon, she even managed to crack a smile at Vernon through the tube.

CHAPTER TWENTY-THREE

John Coltrane's music bounced off of ruby walls and copper floors. Premium coffee poured from a metallic machine into Styrofoam cups. Patrons stood in line with their wallets out as their bodies moved to the music.

Emerald occupied one of the round tables toward the back of the coffee shop. The steam from her coffee faded into the sunlight as she read an article about the war from the local newspaper. She took a sip of her coffee and stared into a powder blue sky with smoky clouds.

"Yeah, girl, I had to go somewhere I could get fed, because Gethsemane was not working."

Emerald looked up and saw Alicia, a member she had not seen in a while, on her cell phone while in line.

"It's like a spirit of depression is on that place," Alicia continued, "and I can't deal with that. I go to Victory Temple now. The pastor there is off the chain, and there are some cuties who go there too."

"Tall latte!" One of the employees called out.

"That's me!" Alicia held up her receipt and walked toward the front of the counter. "Girl, got to go. I'll see you tonight at Zazoos. Remember, it's free before ten." Alicia hung up her phone and walked out with her coffee in hand.

Emerald wanted to follow behind her and snatch her by her neck and choke her. "Lord, forgive me," she apologized for her thoughts.

A gray mini-van pulled up into a parking spot outside of the coffee shop. She recognized the "I Love Jesus" bumper sticker as Renee got out of the car. She wore a sundress with maroon sunshades that sat on top of her head.

When Renee first walked into the coffee shop, she stood in line. She scanned the room and gave Emerald a pleasant wave. Several minutes passed before Renee received her order. She then walked over to Emerald.

"Hey, girl, thanks for coming on such short notice." Emerald took another sip of her coffee.

"You know I need my coffee in the morning, so it was not a problem." Renee set her coffee on the table.

"Did you get your usual?"

"You know me, a creature of habit. I got to have my triple-shot latte with soy." Renee took a sip of her coffee. "Ma'am?"

"I just stick to my white mocha." Emerald folded her newspaper and put it away.

"I stopped reading the newspaper and watching the news. It's too negative."

"Tell me about it."

"So what's going on?"

"Look, Renee, the last several months have been tough on our entire ministry." Emerald set down her cup of coffee. "I know you believe that Dennis should've been the senior pastor, but we have to have faith in God and in Pastor Jones's decision to give the church over to Timothy."

"I know, but it's unfair. My husband has served this ministry for years, and he has never said no to Pastor, and he has never complained. I just can't understand why Ananias would not want him to be pastor."

"I know, but this was not something Timothy campaigned for, and the last thing I wanted to be was the First Lady. But that's the path God has laid before me and my husband, and I know that a divided house will not stand."

"What's that supposed to mean?"

"Renee, we all have to give an account for what we've done on this earth, and I know that you do not want trying to turn a church against its pastor on your record. If God called for Dennis to be pastor of his own church, then He will make a way for him, just like he made a way for my husband."

"I'm not so sure about that now." Renee put her head down and took a sip of coffee.

"I love you, Renee, and I don't want to throw away our friendship, but I do plan to give my husband all of the love and support he needs, and I ask that you and your husband support us. We would do the same if the roles were reversed." Emerald reached for Renee's hand.

"Fine." Renee did not make eye contact with Emerald.

"I miss us getting together like this." Emerald leaned back and stared out the window.

"So do I." Renee took another sip from her coffee.

"I still plan to call you for our annual Easter shopping spree." Emerald smiled.

"I'll be waiting." Renee took another sip before she looked at her watch. "I have to go. Got plenty of errands to run."

"Okay, girl, I'll call you later on in the week."

Emerald did not leave the coffee shop when Renee left; instead, she sat at her table and once again watched as the steam from her coffee disappeared in the sunlight.

For the first time in months, Constance was home alone on a Saturday night. She ran through two pints of cherry ice cream and was halfway through a Lifetime movie marathon when she turned the channel to a popular music station.

Constance watched a music video, which took place inside of a club. The girls dry-humped the guys. She remembered when she used to live carefree like the girls in the video. Before she got saved, Constance would go to the club at least twice a week. Some places did not even bother to ask her for ID.

Constance loved the instrumental to the song and she felt like dancing, so she decided to give her friend from work, Angela, a call. Angela was an avid club person.

"Hello," Angela answered her phone.

"Hey, girl, it's me, Constance."

"Hey, girl, how you doing?"

"Done had a long day. I need to go somewhere and take my mind off my problems."

"Well, I was going to go to Club Eclipse later on tonight."

"Where's that club at?"

"Downtown off of Second and Stutter Ave."

"I thought that was where Club Nubian used to be."

"Girl, when's the last time you've been to the club? It ain't been called Club Nubian in years."

"You think you could pick me up? I don't feel like driving."

"Sure, momma, I'll be there at ten-thirty."

"Okay, cool!" Constance looked at her watch and saw that it was 9:26 PM. She only had a little bit of time to get ready for the world.

The music from the speakers intensified Constance's heartbeat. Neon lights rotated on the dance floor of Club Eclipse while the deejay mixed hip-hop with up-tempo R&B.

The bar was filled with patrons who nodded their heads to the beat and mouthed the lyrics to the songs in between sips of alcohol. Constance wore a dress two sizes too small. Her curvaceous body made her the object of both envy and desire. She sat at the bar with her second glass of Hennessy in hand and started to feel the effects of the alcohol. Constance had not had a drink in years, so her alcohol tolerance was low.

"You need to get a shot of Hypno." Angela held out a glass with an aqua blue substance.

"Naw, girl, I stick to my Coke and Hennessy, but tonight it's going to be straight Hennessy." Constance took a sip and let the alcohol burn down her throat before it sizzled in her stomach.

"Girl, I had drama at home," Angela said.

"Tell me about it."

"Mom's mad that she had to watch my son. Complaining that I go out too much. But I'm twenty-seven. What I'm supposed to do? Sit in the house?"

"I didn't know you had a kid!" Constance asked, puzzled.

"Yeah, Hector is going to be two in March. You didn't see the pictures on my desk?"

"I never noticed them, and I don't recall you ever mentioning him either."

Constance's days consisted of boardroom meetings with Jewel Marketing Firm and studio sessions. On average, she operated with four hours of sleep.

"I had an abortion when I was sixteen. My mom's a strict Catholic, so when I got pregnant again, I decided to keep it. I'm not trying to go hell."

"Is the father in the picture?" Constance asked.

"Heck naw. That loser lives down the street and barely sees his son. He doesn't work, so I can't collect child support."

"That's a shame."

"It sure is!" Angela set her drink down on the table. "Come on, momma, let's dance."

"Oh no, I'm just going to sit here and sip on my drink."

"Well, I'm about to go look for my future ex-husband." Angela winked as she adjusted her top.

"Happy hunting!" Constance called out.

Angela disappeared into an oasis of outstretched arms and vibrant bodies. The deejay slowed down the music to an erotic song, and partners of both opposite and same sex pulled each other close as they grinded to the music.

"You are too fine to be sitting alone."

Constance turned around and faced a tall, clean-cut, light-skinned brother with green eyes who she knew spelled trouble. "Now I remember another reason why I stopped going to the club," she mumbled under her breath.

"What you drinking on?" he asked.

He flashed a smile as bright as his skin. Constance preferred the chocolate type, but for him, she was willing to make an exception. "Hennessy."

"If you drinking Hennessy straight, then that means you're not drinking socially."

"Exactly, so why don't you go run your tired lines to someone else? If you want, I could point out a few candidates for you," Constance said with drink in hand. She scanned the rest of the bar.

"Oh, you got jokes."

"I just don't got time to play any games."

"I'm not trying to play games, ma. I just want to talk with you, buy you a drink."

"I'll take the drink," Constance said before she let out a laugh.

"You a cold piece, ma. I'm Romel." He extended his hand.

"Claudette." It was a fake name and persona she used to use back in the days. Constance extended her hand like a debutante.

"Now, can I buy you that drink?"

"Sure."

Romel signaled to the bartender to refill both his and Constance's drinks. With a nice build and no sign of a wedding band on his finger, Constance's interest increased.

"Here you go, m'lady," Romel said with a smile.

"Thank you." Constance sipped from the thin red straw that accompanied her drink.

"Long day?" Romel asked.

"I guess you can say that."

"Yeah, I had to go in the office today and finish up some work. I hate working on the weekend."

"Where do you work?"

"Image software. And you?"

"I work for an advertising firm."

"Okay, that's cool."

Constance's attraction to Romel grew. She tried to guess his age. She figured that he was not much older than twenty-five. She did not date men younger than her, and even though she was only three years older, Constance could not afford to lower her standards. At the same time, there was no harm in a conversation.

"Can I buy you another one?" Romel asked.

"Yes, but this is going to be my last drink."

Constance woke up the next morning in an unfamiliar room with her bra as the only article of clothing on her body and a massive headache.

Her saliva had a sour taste. She turned to find Romel asleep with his back turned to her. There was a tattoo of a lion on his right shoulder. She momentarily rested her head on a black silk pillow. She drew her attention to the vanity mirror in his bedroom, which rivaled the size of his TV, and the assortment of colognes and massage oils. She could only imagine what had taken place last night.

Constance sat up and stepped on a broken condom wrapper. She slid off the bed and started to get dressed, but her weight lifting off the mattress awakened Romel.

"So you're going to leave before I get a chance to make my world famous pancakes?" he asked.

"Look, Romeo . . ."

"Romel."

"Whatever. Last night was a mistake. I just got out of a bad relationship, and I'm not interested in getting into another one."

"Okay, well, I'm not interested in a relationship either, Claudette. But I was thinking that we could at least kick it."

"I'm a Christian. I don't normally get down like this, but I made a mistake, and I would appreciate it if we just forget about last night."

"Well, it's kind of hard to forget about last night, but I see how it is. You didn't have a problem with me when we were getting down, but today you're on some other stuff."

"Don't talk to me like you know me." Constance pointed her finger at Romel. "You don't know what's going on in my life, so don't sit there and judge me."

"Man, whatever. If you want to leave, then leave. No one's holding you hostage."

Constance gathered the rest of her clothes and stormed out of the apartment and down a flight of stairs. She stumbled in her heels, but regained her balance. Her body felt like someone had poured honey all over it. She wanted to go home and wash away the dirty, sticky feeling she had. She got outside of Romel's apartment and noticed the street sign read Powell and El Camino Real. She grabbed her cell phone and called Angela.

"Hello?" Angela answered.

"Hey, girl, how are you?" Constance asked.

"How are you is the question. Last time I saw you, you were kissing some hot guy, and then you told me not to worry about giving you a ride home."

"Actually, now I do need a ride home."

"Was it that bad?"

"To tell you the truth, I can't remember."

"That's a yes. Umm, I'm actually at my nephew's baseball game. I can pick you up afterwards."

"That's okay. I'll catch a cab."

"You sure?"

"Yeah, don't worry about it."

"Well, call me later, okay?"

"Okay, girl."

Constance hung up the phone and decided to walk along the train tracks that led to a light rail station. The sun stretched behind the cumulous clouds. The dew drops sat on top of the wet green grass, and the birds soared from the trees to a nearby telephone pole. Constance could not appreciate the beautiful morning. In a short breath of time, everything that meant anything to her was reduced to rubble. Now within the crevices of her soul, she searched for a reason not to commit suicide.

The prescription bottle said to take only two every four hours. Constance had poured a handful of pills in one hand and held a bottle of vodka in her other hand. She presumed that this was the most painless way to go. She hoped to drift off into a deep sleep and awake in heaven. Constance also rationalized it was justice for her unborn child; an eye for an eye.

Lightheaded from the sight of the half-white, half-red pills, Constance scooted down to the edge of her bed.

Satan emerged. *Go ahead, end your suffering, God will understand. Why live in misery?*

"Lord Jesus, help me."

With tears in her eyes, Constance looked up and walked over to her daily scripture calendar. Normally, Constance used the calendar to mark off the days of the month, but today's verse was taken from Titus 3:5. "He saved us, not because of righteous things we had done, but because of his mercy."

Constance could not dismiss that scripture as mere coincidence. She walked over to the mirror that hung on her closet doors and confronted the person she did not want to face. Her face was flushed with tears, but she did not see a murderer. The pills slid from her hand like a waterfall onto the floor.

"Thank you, Jesus!"

CHAPTER TWENTY-FOUR

Her eyes resembled almonds and her skin was a golden brown. Her hair was as black as soot. Without a full set of teeth, her smile rendered everyone helpless. Layla fit within the palms of Timothy's hands.

"In the Book of Samuel, Hannah dedicated her first child, Samuel, to God, and that is why we're here now, to dedicate Eric and Rochelle's first child, Layla, to God."

Layla's godparents and family surrounded Timothy. He placed oil on her forehead and held her up in the air.

"Father, in the name of Jesus, we ask that you watch over Layla right now and that you bless her to have a healthy, Godly life, and may everyone who bears witness today to Layla's dedication make every effort to love her, nourish her, and bring her up in the ways of God. In Jesus' name, we pray. Amen."

"Amen," a handful of the congregants said.

As Timothy posed for a picture with Layla's family, he noticed a woman who resembled Constance, with the exception of the fact that the woman did not wear any makeup and she wore just a white T-shirt and sweatpants. Constance always dressed her best for God.

"May God bless you and keep you," Timothy said to a congregation before he handed the microphone to Pastor Childs to give the benediction.

"That was a beautiful ceremony," Emerald said as she and Timothy walked toward the church entrance.

"I know. She was so tiny and adorable sitting in my hands," Timothy replied.

"You're going to be a great father," Emerald said.

"One day, but not anytime soon."

Timothy and Emerald greeted members of the congregation and exchanged pleasantries on their way out the door. Several minutes passed before Constance appeared and Timothy realized that Constance was the same woman who came in church in a T-shirt and sweatpants.

"Constance, we've missed you," Emerald said.

"I know." Constance averted her eyes.

"Are you okay?" Emerald asked with her hand on Constance's arm.

"Actually, I'm not." She then looked to Timothy. "I was wondering if I could talk to you in private."

"Sure, sure." Timothy gave Emerald a head nod.

On Timothy and Constance's walk back to Timothy's office, they passed by Renee, who had just walked out of children's church. Timothy had offered Renee the position of Sunday school teacher when the previous teacher resigned and went to another church.

"Hello, Pastor," Renee said.

"Hello, God bless you. How was Sunday school?" Timothy replied.

"Great!"

"Good to hear."

They entered Timothy's office, and Timothy removed his

jacket and placed it on the door hook. He loosened his tie and unbuttoned the top button.

"Can I offer you something to drink?" Timothy opened the door of his mini refrigerator and removed a bottle of water.

"No, thank you, Pastor." Constance took a seat in front of Timothy's desk.

"So what's going on?" Timothy asked after he took a sip of water and sat down at his desk.

"Pastor, I feel like I'm losing my mind."

"Is it the pressure from the album?"

"The album is the least of my problems. Besides, my album has been shelved."

"Why? Every time I talked to you it seemed like everything was going great."

Constance buried her face in her lap and began to rock back and forth. "I had an abortion six months ago." Constance lifted her head up from her lap and brushed her hair back with her hand. "I didn't tell anyone except for a co-worker."

"What about the father?"

"He doesn't even know. I couldn't tell him. I've had girlfriends whose men did not respond well to unexpected pregnancies. Besides, I thought it would destroy my career. I ended up doing that myself."

"Why didn't you go to Pastor Jones about this?"

"No! I didn't want him thinking any less of me, so I had the abortion anyway, and I've lived in torment ever since. It took everything I had not to kill myself. I had to run out the house and get here to see you." Constance started to cry.

"God is punishing me, and I feel like it's selfish of me to ask for forgiveness. That's why I haven't been coming to church, because I feel like such a hypocrite when I come here." Constance wiped the tears from her eyes with a white tissue.

Timothy walked over to Constance and removed her hands from her eyes. After a moment, she looked up. Behind her bloodshot red eyes was a broken child of God who just wanted freedom.

"The church was not built for those who have their life in order, but for people like you and me who often mess up and need God's help. This should be the last place where you feel guilty. Do you understand me?"

"But what I did was so horrible, and I can't fix it."

"That's why Jesus died for our sins, so you wouldn't have to carry that burden. All you have to do is just ask God for His forgiveness."

Constance began to wipe her face. "I wish I had a chance to make it right."

"You can't. Life moves forward. We have to give it to God and let Him repair the things that are broken in our lives. I'm not excusing what you did; I'm just saying it's time to let God have this situation and it's time for you to move on."

"I'm so sorry, Pastor."

"You don't have to apologize to me, but I want you to take some time to reconnect with God. I want to see you back in church, okay?"

"Okay." Constance cracked a smile.

Timothy gave Constance a hug. He was aware that the gesture might be inappropriate, but he didn't know what else to do. The hug was more paternal than anything else, but at that moment, Timothy knew his value as a pastor.

CHAPTER TWENTY-FIVE

Since his sermon, Dennis had cut off all lines of communication with Renee, and she did not know why. He barely spoke to her and was always on the defensive. Even the kids seemed intimidated by their father.

Renee walked into the bedroom and found Dennis curled up on his side of the bed. His Bible had remained at the edge of his nightstand from the time he had come home last Sunday after delivering the message, and had not moved since.

"Is everything okay?" she asked.

"I'm fine." Dennis did not turn over.

"No, you're not."

"Don't start, Renee. I'm trying to get some sleep."

"Did I do something wrong? Tell me."

"Why would you say that?" Dennis finally turned around.

"Since last Sunday, you've barely touched me, and you've treated me as if I was the source of your problems. I thought you did a good job. I thought your sermon was excellent."

"No, it wasn't. It lacked the anointing."

"Oh, nonsense. You're an anointed preacher. People were

being touched and delivered." Renee lay next to Dennis and rubbed his chest.

"They cried, they danced, and they shouted at the altar because that is what they do every week." Dennis brushed away Renee's hand. "I could've been speaking in gibberish, and it wouldn't have mattered. They still would have cried and shouted and danced, because they don't know how to do anything else."

Renee was terrified by the look on her husband's face. He appeared to be on the verge of tears.

"Honey, what's wrong?"

Dennis got out of bed and walked to the rear bedroom window. He opened the blinds and the moonlight pierced through the blinds. Renee loved when the moon resembled a fingertip. Something was wrong with her husband, and she started to doubt whether it had anything to do with his sermon.

"I've committed a great sin against you and God." Dennis turned around. "I had an affair."

Renee did not believe Dennis. She knew he was serious, but she could not figure out how, or with whom. She kept a close watch of the women at church and did not suspect any of them.

"I had an affair with Cecilia, my assistant. Last week, I kissed her when I was working late."

Renee's emotions caused the veins in her hands and forehead to throb. She lunged at Dennis and swung wildly at him. Her first blow grazed his forehead, while the second blow connected with his face as his skin got underneath her fingernails.

Dennis tried to restrain Renee, but she resisted like a jackrabbit.

"Let go of me!" Renee screamed.

"Calm down, baby." Dennis squeezed Renee close to his body.

"No!" Renee broke loose and fell upon the bed with her strength sapped. She was barely able to draw a healthy breath.

"Baby, breathe," Dennis said as he patted Renee on the back.

"Mommy, Daddy!" Elijah banged on the door.

Renee got off the bed and tried to regain her breath as she walked over to the door and opened it. Both Elijah and Jasmine were in their pajamas. Jasmine held a teddy bear in her arms.

"Go to bed. Everything is okay," Renee assured the children.

Renee turned the children around and gave them a slight shove. She closed the door and turned around to see Dennis still in the same position.

"I have done everything for you, everything you asked, and I barely got anything in return. But I didn't complain. But that wasn't enough for you. You had to go have an affair with another woman."

"I didn't have sex with her. I stopped before we got a chance to even go that far."

Renee tried to slap Dennis again, but he caught her hand.

"You make me sick. I've been fighting for you and for what? For what? Answer me!" Renee landed a slap on Dennis's face and Dennis balled a fist.

"Go ahead. You've done everything else. You're a hypocrite! A straight-up hypocrite. I'm glad that you're not the pastor."

Dennis brushed past Renee and went into the closet, and a second later, he came out with a jacket in hand.

"Not even man enough to stay and fight for our marriage." Renee stood in Dennis's way.

"Move, Renee."

"No. You're going to stay and talk."

Dennis pushed Renee onto the bed and slammed the door. Seconds later, Renee heard the front door slam. Renee drove her fist into the pillow and followed with a series of combinations as if she were in a boxing match, until she was too tired to fight.

Emerald had only been to Renee's house on a few occasions, but never at night. The neighborhood was poorly lit and the lanes were so narrow that Emerald found it hard to keep from crossing the yellow dividing line. She even overshot Renee's house and had to make a three-point turn to go back.

Emerald parked her car and walked slowly up the driveway to the door. She rang the loud doorbell.

"Hello, Mrs. Wells," Elijah said as he opened the door.

"Hello, handsome," Emerald replied.

Emerald followed Elijah into the living room where Renee was sitting.

"Thank you for getting the door, sweetie. Now go to bed, okay," Renee said while she rubbed Elijah's head.

"Is Daddy going to come home?" Elijah said before exiting the room.

"Of course he will, baby, but you don't want him to catch you still up when he gets home, do you?" Renee gave Elijah a pat on the butt as he went into his bedroom. She then turned her attention to her company. "Thank you for coming over. I really didn't know who to talk to."

"Oh, sure, girl. What's going on?"

Renee double-checked to see that the kids' bedroom door was closed. Once confirmed, Renee let out a deep sigh. "Dennis had an affair."

Emerald put her hands over her mouth to conceal her shock.

"When did this happen?"

"Last week. He said that all he did was kiss her, but I'm not sure I believe that, and I don't know how long this has been going on. I've done everything within my power to be a good, Godly wife to Dennis, and this is the thanks I get?"

Emerald took a seat next to Renee on the couch. She placed Renee's head on her shoulder.

"I want to hate him so much for what he did. But I can't, because I love him too much."

"I don't know all that happened, but if he stopped at a kiss, then maybe it was his love for you that stopped him."

"He swore himself to me and me only. He vowed to give himself to me, then he broke that vow."

"And you vowed for better or for worse."

"So what? Am I supposed to let him get away with kissing another woman?" Renee removed her head from Emerald's shoulder.

"I didn't say that, but you have to make up your mind whether or not this is worth ending your marriage. I don't know; only you know that."

"I was raised in a single home, and I do not want that for my kids."

"My parents raised me, but they didn't like each other very much. There are no guarantees in love.

"Let's have some tea." Emerald got up and went into the kitchen, opened cabinets, and pulled out a pot. She searched until she found the tea. Renee took a seat at the kitchen table.

"He called Timothy not too long after you called me. He'll be home because Timothy knows that I want his butt home."

"Do you ever wonder about your husband?"

Emerald knew Renee could not be miserable alone. She sought an opportunity to get information, and that did not sit well for Emerald.

"What do you mean?" Emerald opened a box of green tea.

"That maybe he's been unfaithful?" Renee walked over to the kitchen table and sat down. She pulled out a deck of cards and started shuffling.

"Are these cups okay?" Emerald held up two royal blue teacups.

"They're perfect."

Emerald put a tea bag into each cup before she sat down in front of Renee. "I admit sometimes I get a little concerned, but then I remember how devastated Timothy was when his father left his mother for another woman. I knew that when he vowed to stay faithful to me, that was exactly what he meant."

A few moments later, the teapot whistled. Emerald got up and turned off the stove and poured the hot water into each cup before she placed two spoons in the cups and brought them over to the table.

"Where do you keep your sugar?" Emerald asked.

"Out of the hands of the children." Renee got up and opened the cabinet above the stove and removed a glass jar filled with sugar. She placed the jar of sugar next to Emerald

"I'm sorry for asking. It's just that I'm so hurt right now, that I don't want to deal with this alone."

"You're not alone. I'm here, and God is here with you." Emerald reached for Renee's hand.

"Thank you." Renee squeezed Emerald's hand.

Dennis's fists bounced off of the concrete wall of Smiley's liquor store. When Timothy arrived, he discovered an open liquor bottle on the ground.

"What's going on, Dennis?" Timothy asked him.

"You know I went almost ten years without a drink. Then I started my company and figured a drink here and there would not hurt. I shouldn't have told her." Dennis began to pace back and forth.

"What happened?"

Dennis picked up the bottle of liquor and took a big swig without any reverence to Timothy's presence.

"I told her that I kissed another woman; my secretary."

"Was it the girl I saw the other day?"

"Yeah, she came in to quit. It wasn't even worth it. It wasn't as if I had sex with her. I would've if I had known Renee was going to react that way."

"You know that this is not the way we solve our problems."

"Don't preach to me." Dennis turned his back on Timothy. "I'm not a hypocrite; I'm not one of these preachers you read about in the news who sleep around with their members, living any ol' kind of way."

"Then don't act like one. Go home and try to reconcile with Renee. Tell her that you made a foolish mistake, and then let God work on your marriage."

"God is so disappointed in me that I'm embarrassed to even ask Him for anything."

"He may be disappointed, but it doesn't mean that you're not His child or that He doesn't love you. We serve a God of restoration."

"What about my position as associate pastor?"

"Don't worry about that. Go home to your family and get your house in order."

Dennis looked down, and in the midst of the cracks in the concrete and chewed gum stuck to the ground, he poured out the liquor and let it bounce off the pavement. Some spilled into the street, while some retreated underneath Dennis's shoes. The rest made a bee-line to the dirt pile.

"Pray for me, Pastor," Dennis said without taking his eyes off the concrete.

Timothy began to pray. When he finished his prayer, nothing was said. The two just leaned against the wall and watched drunken college students stumble their way home.

"Let me give you a ride home." Timothy reached in his pocket and grabbed his keys.

Dennis tossed the bottle in a trashcan next to the newspaper stand and walked to Timothy's car.

*   *   *

Emerald slept with the TV on until Timothy came in and turned on the closet light next to the bedroom. It was around the time when infomercials dominated the airwaves.

"Did you talk to him?" Emerald yawned.

"Yes," an exhausted Timothy said.

"So what happened?"

"He kissed another woman; his secretary."

"I know. Renee told me." Emerald sat up.

Timothy sat on the edge of the bed with his back to his wife.

"What's wrong, baby?" Emerald asked.

"He and his wife have conspired against me this whole time, and all I've done is obey God. As Dennis was telling me what happened, there was a part of me that got pleasure for his suffering. I felt like he had gotten what he deserved."

Emerald knew Timothy's mindset, because she battled with the same emotions earlier at Renee's house. She crawled over to Timothy and rested her head on his shoulder blades and started to rub his arms.

"You're human, babe. You're human."

"I know, but I'm a pastor. I'm not supposed to wish anything bad on other people."

"Baby, you've been under a lot of pressure, and I'm just glad that all you had was a feeling. You've handled yourself well these last few months."

"At first I did not want to be a pastor, and I would've been grateful if they would've found someone to replace me, but sitting in that board meeting a few weeks ago, everything within me was fighting to keep the ministry, because I know that I may not be the first choice, but I do know my love for God is genuine."

"So what are you going to do about Dennis?"

"I don't know. I was thinking about going to see Ananias and get his advice."

Emerald kissed the back of Timothy's neck and began to rub his chest.

"Baby, come to bed."

"I can't. I still have papers to grade and I haven't even started on my sermon for Sunday. There's just not enough hours in the day."

Emerald released her hold on Timothy and crawled back to her side of the bed. She got underneath the covers and turned on her right side. "The papers can wait. I need you."

Timothy lay down and Emerald rested her head on his chest.

"It feels like sometimes I'll never catch up," Timothy said.

"You will, baby. You just got to give it to God."

"You're right."

Emerald took her finger and drew designs on Timothy's chest. Timothy kissed the crown of her head and ran his fingers through her hair.

"Baby, I saw the cutest little boy today," Emerald said.

"Oh, really?"

"Yeah. He was decked out in his Jordans and basketball jersey."

"Humph."

"I want us to have a son."

"Yeah, but not anytime soon. The timing is off."

"The timing isn't going to ever be right." Emerald slapped Timothy on his chest.

"Just give it a year."

"I'm almost thirty. The more I wait, the more I'm at risk."

Emerald pulled the covers close to her. Timothy tried to hold Emerald, but she fought his hand away. "Good night, Pastor."

When Dennis got home, all the lights were turned off. It was cold and quiet. He could not make out any images in the dark. He saw two blankets and a pillow on top of the couch.

"You've got to be kidding me."

Dennis went to his bedroom door and tried to turn the knob. It was locked. He knocked on the door, but there was no answer. He didn't even hear a sound from his kids' room. Dennis checked the closet next to the bathroom and all blankets had been removed. He went back into the living room and lay on the couch.

Most days Dennis dreaded going home to his wife and kids, but tonight, he would do anything to be in the warm bed with his wife. He wondered if there would ever again come a time when he could sleep with his wife in peace.

CHAPTER TWENTY-SIX

When they arrived home from court, the manager had taped a three-day notice on the outside of their door. Kristal snatched the notice off the door and went into the apartment. She tossed the notice on the coffee table and Vernon took off his navy blue blazer and laid it on the couch. He loosened his tie as he went to the refrigerator.

One whiff of the milk and Vernon's stomached turned. Still in the dress shirt and red tie he had worn to court, Vernon had poured a bowl of both a fruity cereal and cornflakes. Vernon got up and rinsed the milk out in the sink. He then poured the cereal into the trashcan.

Vernon managed to peek at the electric bill with a yellow strip across the top and the words "48-hour notice" written in bold, black letters. The balance due on the bill was $128.78. He went to the refrigerator and shuffled around some of the food.

"Are you hungry, baby?" Kristal asked Vernon.

"No, I'm okay."

Kristal closed the refrigerator door and opened the top

cabinet next to the stove. She shook a box of macaroni and cheese and left it on the counter. Kristal went over by the trashcan and noticed the cereal at the top.

"Boy, what I tell you about wasting food?"

"The milk smelled funny, Mom."

"Funny? That's why you're skinny now."

Autumn stayed with one of Kristal's friends while Vernon and his mother were in court. Autumn's recovery was a miracle. She was as energetic as ever, and Vernon could not be more pleased. Vernon did not understand this God that Mr. Wells believed in. But he knew that if God prevented his sister from dying, then maybe he could prevent them from being homeless.

"Mom, I want to go to Mr. Wells' church on Sunday," Vernon told his mother.

"I don't know, sweetie. We'll see."

"I made God a promise that I would go to church."

"Sweetie, God understands. Besides, you're not supposed to make promises like that."

"I know, but He kept His promise. The least I can do is keep mines."

"Sweetie, right now I got a lot more things on my mind than going to church; like trying to keep a roof over our heads."

"Ask Mr. Wells."

"Mr. Wells has done enough. I don't want to keep bothering him."

Kristal closed Autumn's room door and walked back to the kitchen. She sat back in the chair and sorted the various medical bills. Vernon entered moments later and sat next to Kristal.

"What's wrong?" Kristal asked.

"They gave Uncle Alex a long time," Vernon said.

"They should've gave him more time for what he did to you."

Vernon heard the judge give his uncle twenty years. That was a long time for anyone to be locked up. Vernon could not believe his uncle pleaded guilty and was happy to get that amount of time. Vernon did not even have to testify, which was a relief.

"He didn't hurt Autumn, Momma, I swear."

"You were very brave, and I couldn't have gone through what you went through. I still don't understand why you didn't tell me."

"I was scared, and he was my uncle. I didn't know if you would believe me. It's all my fault that Autumn got hit by a car."

Kristal started to cry, and she pulled Vernon close and kissed him on the forehead. "Listen to me. It's not your fault. You were protecting your sister. You have nothing to feel ashamed of."

Vernon still shouldered the guilt. If he had said something sooner, none of this would have happened, but he allowed his uncle to put fear in his heart and silence his words.

"I'm going to need you to watch your sister for me until I get back, okay?"

"I will, Mom."

"Do you want me to bring you something back?"

"A strawberry milkshake."

"Okay, I won't make any promises."

Kristal gave Vernon a hug until the doorbell rang. She opened the door and Greg was on the other side in a traditional scrubs uniform.

"What's going on, shorty?"

"Hey." Kristal kissed Greg.

"You ready?" Greg asked.

"Yeah, just let me get my coat." Kristal held the door open

for Greg and she sprinted into her bedroom, leaving Greg alone with Vernon. Greg's girth was similar to Alex's, and he liked to touch too much for Vernon's comfort.

"What's up, little man?" Greg reached to rub Vernon's head.

Vernon moved out of the way. He stood still with his eyes nailed to Greg's chest.

"Vernon, what's wrong with you?" Greg said.

Kristal came in and noticed Vernon's awkward reaction to Greg. She rushed over to Vernon and snapped him out of his trance.

"Go in your room and finish your homework, okay, sweetie?"

Kristal gave Vernon a kiss on the forehead, then ushered him out of the kitchen. But Vernon never went to his room; instead, he hid on the other side of the wall to eavesdrop.

"What's wrong with him?" Greg asked.

"Nothing, he's fine," Kristal said.

"You must be putting the belt to him."

"I don't whip my kids."

"That's what you need to start doing. The kids wouldn't act up so much."

"Don't tell me how to raise my kids."

"Okay, Sister Souljah, you ain't got to bite my head off."

"I'm sorry. I just got a lot on my mind. I'm short on rent, and I was hoping that maybe you could help me out this one time."

"How short are you?"

"I need four hundred dollars." Kristal rubbed her head.

"Whew! I wish I could help you out, but I just got finished paying rent myself. The best I could do is give you two hundred, but I wouldn't have the other two until next week. When's your rent due?"

"It was due yesterday. Just like everybody else's."

"I don't know what to tell you. You're going to have pray

or go to the pawn shop or something. I'll give you two hundred, though."

Vernon knew two hundred dollars was not enough, and his suggestion of going to Mr. Wells for help was not as silly as it seemed.

Timothy sat at his desk and gazed at the blank yellow tablet.

"Lord, what do you want me to say to your people?"

There was a knock on the door, and then Emerald entered.

"Babe, you have back-to-back meetings with Deacon Robinson and Mr. Blake," Emerald informed as she handed Timothy a handful of papers.

"I don't know what I was thinking when I made back-to-back appointments," Timothy conveyed as he sorted through the papers and made the necessary adjustments.

"Yeah, and there's someone in the lobby to see you as well."

"Who?" Timothy probed.

"Someone named Kristal."

Timothy's countenanced changed. He unrolled his sleeves and buttoned the cuffs. "This is going to be a long day."

Timothy reached the lobby to find Kristal in a pair of jeans and a tank top with "Brat" written on the front.

"Good morning, Ms. Williams." Timothy extended his hand.

"Hello, Pastor Wells." Kristal shook his hand.

"Let's talk in my office."

Kristal followed Timothy to his office. Timothy opened the door and allowed Kristal to go in first before he closed the door behind him. Kristal took a seat and placed her purse on the arm of the chair.

"I spoke to your attorney last week, and I told him that I was willing to testify."

"Yeah, about that, there's not going to be a trial. My brother pleaded guilty to all counts and got a reduced sentence."

Timothy sat down in his chair and put his hands on top of his head. "Well, I'm glad that you guys don't have to go through a drawn-out trial."

"No. My brother is going to be locked up for a very long time. They gave him twenty years."

"How's Autumn?"

"She'll be running around soon. The cast is off, and her bones healed nicely."

"Praise God. That's good news. Vernon has written about his sister frequently in his daily journals."

"He's a good brother."

"So, how may I help you?"

"Well, Vernon is also a good son, and he suggested that I come to you for help."

"Okay."

"I'm short on the rent for this month, and if I don't have rent in full by the end of the day, we're going to be put out. I'm also about to have my lights cut off, and to have a daughter in a cast without a place to stay, that's pretty hard."

"Have you asked anyone for help?"

"No one can help us. Besides, I couldn't afford to pay anybody back no ways."

"How short are you on rent?"

"Two hundred for rent, not to mention I need at least one hundred to keep the lights on."

Timothy leaned back in his chair. "I wish we could help, but we would need at least a couple of business days to cut a check, and it's too late in the afternoon."

"I understand." Kristal put her head down.

"I'm sorry."

Moments later, Kristal lifted her head. "You know, I thought that this was a place of miracles. Well, here I am, hoping you could bless me with a miracle, and what do I get? Nothing! I guess I have to be a member to get help."

"We've helped people in the past who weren't members and were in similar circumstances." Timothy leaned forward on his desk and put his hands together.

"You know my son looks up to you. He's young and foolish. He still believes in heroes. But I know better, and I'm sorry for wasting your time." Kristal stood up and put her purse on her shoulder.

"Wait." Timothy stood up. "Vernon is not foolish for believing in heroes, and I would expect you to be an example to him of what a hero is."

"So what are you trying to say, I'm a bad mother?"

"I didn't say that, but you need to stop blaming yourself for what happened. It's not your fault that your brother turned out the way he did, but you have two precious children who need their mother to be strong for them."

"Thank you. I come for some help, and I get a sermon. You have a nice day, Pastor."

Kristal walked out of Timothy's office. Timothy did not know what to say, but he knew that he did not want her to leave with those negative thoughts.

"Are you okay?" Emerald poked her head through the door after seeing Kristal make her swift exit.

"Yeah, I'm fine." Timothy returned back to his desk.

"God seems to be bringing them in one after the other. Deacon Robinson is in the lobby."

"Okay. Listen, how much do we have in the benevolence fund?"

Emerald let out a laugh. "We exhausted that months ago when we helped Sister Vickie with her rent, and we haven't been able to replenish it because of the increase of our own rent."

"Well, we'll talk about it later. In the meantime, send Deacon Robinson in."

Timothy repositioned himself at his desk when Deacon Robinson walked in with a tan Kangol hat in hand.

"Good morning, Pastor." Deacon Robinson extended his hand.

"How's everything, Deacon Robinson?" Timothy released the handshake and sat back down at his desk.

"I can't complain."

"How may I help you, Deacon?"

"Well, I'm not going to beat around the bush. I think it's time I pack up and head out." Deacon sat in the brown chair across from Timothy's desk.

"Really? What brought this on?"

"Pastor, when you took over, I was very skeptical. When I saw a lot of people leave, I really became concerned, but I have to admit that I think you've done a pretty decent job as pastor. I just can't continue to go on in the same direction that this church is heading in."

"What direction is that?" Timothy asked with his head titled to the side.

"You preached a sermon the other day on tithes and offerings, and even though I know the church is in a financial situation, I can't support a money ministry."

"We're not becoming a money ministry. Tithing is a Biblical principle; if folks have a problem with tithing, then they have a problem with the Bible."

"Now, don't get all defensive, Pastor. I know tithing is a Biblical principal, but folks are struggling, and the last thing they need to hear when they go to church is the preacher talk about money."

Timothy shifted in his seat, folded his hands, and placed his elbows on his desk. "Deacon Robinson, it's incumbent upon me to teach the Bible. Not just the parts that everyone is comfortable with, but the parts that make people uncomfortable. That means subjects like hell and tithing. My concern is for the growth and development of my members, and I can't have my members ignorant simply because money is a touchy subject."

Deacon Robinson stood up with his hat in hand. "Look, Pastor, I didn't come here to argue with you. I came to tell you thank you and that I will be keeping you in my prayers."

Timothy stood up and walked around to shake Deacon Robinson's hand.

"You've been a pillar to this church for so many years. You will be missed."

"I'm sure our paths will cross again. Take care now." Deacon Robinson closed the door behind him.

Timothy fell back into his chair and closed his eyes. The warmth of the heater in his office soothed him so much that he slipped out of consciousness until there was another knock on the door.

"Yes," Timothy said with his eyes still closed.

"Deacon Robinson told me good-bye." Emerald closed the door behind her.

"Yes, he came in and told me that he's leaving."

"I wish I could say I was surprised, but I'm not."

"Surprised that he hadn't left sooner. I wish I could cancel my meeting with Mr. Blake"

"You can't. He says he's going out of town on a business trip and this can not wait until he gets back."

"Fine. Listen, I'm going to need a big favor from you later."

"Okay, let me know."

Emerald gave Timothy a kiss on the cheek and exited his office. Timothy could not sever his thoughts, from the meeting with Mr. Blake to Deacon Robinson's resignation to Kristal's plea for help. For fifteen minutes, he drew a blank on a topic for his sermon. Another five minutes passed, and then there was another knock on the door.

"Come in," Timothy said.

Mr. Blake entered Timothy's office with a white polo shirt and black slacks on. "Hey, Timothy, I'm getting ready to get on a plane to Colorado this afternoon, but I wanted to stop by and tell you that I talked to a buddy of mine. The buddy has a piece of property that has been vacant for a few years now. He's willing to make you an offer on the building."

"Well, we're not looking for a building, Mr. Blake," Timothy said with a smug look.

"Look, Timothy, I admire your vigilance, but you're fighting an uphill battle."

"We have upheld our end of the deal by paying the rent on time this month."

"Yes, but my guy is willing to offer his property to you for seven thousand dollars a month. It's a smaller venue, but I think I can manage to get him to bring the price down to around sixty-five hundred."

"I'm sorry for wasting your time, but the church is staying right here."

"Timothy, you need to look at this from a business standpoint. I know you Christians believe in blind faith, but I urge you to reconsider."

Mr. Blake sat down on Timothy's couch and clapped his hands together in a praying manner. "I'm not a very religious person, but I do know that as a man of God, you do not want financial burdens. Don't let pride get in the way of making a decision that is best for you and your people."

"I won't. I thank you for stopping by, and I would like to pray for you to have a safe trip to Colorado." Timothy stood up, prepared to pray.

"That's quite all right, Pastor."

Timothy sat back down in his chair and looked at his yellow tablet. He hoped that words could emerge from the blue lines and form a sermon that could bring glory to the kingdom, but for now, too many issues clouded his thoughts.

* * *

Vernon and his mom made quality time with reruns of *The Cosby Show*. His mom shared her fantasies of how she wished they were as rich as the Huxtables. If they were, he and his sister could have anything they wanted. At the same time, he shared his fantasy that she won the lottery and quit her job. Vernon found so much bliss in their fantasies that he did not realize that someone was at the front door.

"Who is it?" Kristal asked as she tied her robe and walked toward the door.

"My name is Emerald Wells; I'm Pastor Wells's wife," Emerald said from the other side of the door.

Kristal opened the door, and Emerald burst through with two bags of groceries in her hands. She wore the same outfit that Kristal had seen her in earlier.

"Girl, these bags are heavy." Emerald repositioned the bags with her knees.

"Oh, come in, come in." Kristal waved Emerald in.

Emerald came in, set the groceries down on the table, and began to unpack them. She put things like eggs, milk, and cheese in the refrigerator.

"What are you doing, Mrs. Wells?" Vernon asked.

"Unpacking groceries." Emerald looked at Vernon "You mind giving me a hand?"

"Yes, Mrs. Wells." Vernon got up and followed her.

"Thank you so much," Kristal said as she went over to the dining room table and started to put groceries away.

"Oh, there's more." Emerald headed toward the door. "You like the Huxtables too?" Emerald pointed at the TV and Kristal nodded her head.

Emerald and Vernon left the apartment only to return minutes later with two more bags of groceries.

"What's all this for?" Kristal asked, still dumbfounded.

"You asked for help, didn't you? Now, I didn't know what

kind of cereal the kids like, so I just bought them some cocoa cereal."

"Thank you, Mrs. Wells," Vernon said.

"You're welcome, pumpkin," Emerald replied.

"Look, Emerald, I'm sorry for blowing up at your husband. I was just frustrated and upset, but all of this ain't necessary."

"Sweetie, why don't you go in your room and play, okay, so your momma and I can talk," Emerald said to Vernon.

"Go 'head, baby," Kristal said with a head nod.

Vernon walked away. Once out of sight, he assumed his position on the other side of the wall where he could hear Emerald and his mother.

"Who you fooling? There's no shame in taking help when it's needed. You got two precious kids and both you and them deserve a break," Emerald scolded.

"I'm getting exactly what I deserve. I left my babies in the hands of a monster and scarred them for life." Kristal pointed toward Autumn's room with her right hand over her heart.

"You are their mother. You have the power to determine whether or not what happens is a scar or a disability."

Kristal's eyes welled up, and without hesitation, Emerald gave her a hug.

"I'm so sorry." Kristal gripped the back of Emerald's jacket.

"It's going to be okay. You don't have anything to worry about." Emerald broke away from Kristal and went into her jacket pocket and pulled out a white envelope.

"Before I forget and accidentally go shopping, here you go." Emerald handed Kristal the envelope. "There's four hundred in there. Hopefully that's enough."

"Thank you." Kristal covered her mouth and cried from joy.

"Thank God. He's the one that put it on our hearts."

* * *

That night, Vernon watched as his mother cooked chicken, rice, and vegetables. It was the first time in a long time that his mother had been able to cook a well-rounded meal. It had been a long time since he had even known where their next meal would come from. But thanks to Gethsemane, he knew where the next few meals would come from. Maybe now his mother could believe in miracles . . . and heroes.

CHAPTER TWENTY-SEVEN

Ananias held the soil in his hands. It looked like chocolate cake crumbs. He planted seeds in efforts to grow some collard greens. He marveled at the thought that some of the most precious things on earth grew from darkness. A seed could be planted deep in the earth, and with just enough light, it could sprout and burst forth.

He was excited by this process because it ran parallel to the growth of Christians. God's light called them out of the darkness of the earth. He was sure that if the Lord ever allowed him to preach another sermon, he would talk about growing out of dark places.

The sound of the doorbell reminded him of his appointment with Timothy. Ananias quickly let the soil fall back into the earth and took off his gloves and made his way to the front of the house.

Timothy looked like a young lion that had come back from his first hunt. His shoulders were broad, and his speech was clear and concise. Ananias could not help but smile at his protégé.

They sat in Ananias's living room, starting a new chess game. Ananias's living room was dark, with the smell of shoe polish and numerous church figurines.

"Now, I know you have not come here just to get beat in a game of chess," Ananias said.

"Pride goes before a fall." Timothy moved his bishop.

"I do not have issue with pride. It's just that people have issues with my confidence."

Ananias found himself in a game in which Timothy was the aggressor. He was not used to being on the defensive, but Timothy caught him off guard with his strategy.

"Dennis cheated on Renee."

Ananias was well aware that Dennis had struggled with the lust of the flesh, but he thought their private counseling sessions had eradicated that desire. Ananias was shocked to find that Dennis's flaws had come to the surface.

"Do you think I should sit Dennis down?" Timothy asked as he looked up from the chessboard.

"Grace is freely given; leadership is earned." Ananias moved his bishop.

"I'm not condoning what he's done, but he made a mistake," Timothy said.

"I would sit him down because he's bringing shame to the cross. He's got a whole lot of issues that he needs to get straight before he starts ministering again."

"He's not going to see it that way. He's going to see it as a punishment."

"But it's not; it's time out of ministry for him to repair his relationship with God and his family."

"Pastor Jones, if it weren't for the grace of God, you and I could've been in the same situation. I'm not going to sit someone down for slipping up, because I'm not above slipping up myself."

"Well, you can do what you want. Just remember that the fellowship always expects more from the leadership."

The next several moves were made in silence.

"You know you could've told me how hard this was going to be."

"And spoil all the fun?" Ananias replied.

"I've missed you," Timothy said.

"I've missed the church so much, but I've gotten a chance to spend time with my family. I even went and saw a movie."

"How was it?"

"It was horrible. The things you kids watch nowadays."

"I haven't been to a movie in a while myself."

"When's the last time you and your wife went out?"

"We haven't had time since I started as pastor. We've been too busy trying to keep the church from going under. But you know Emerald, she understands." Timothy made a move.

"Timothy, I've never given you bad advice, so I hope that you'll heed what I'm about to say."

"Okay."

"Don't get your priorities mixed up. I miss Helen now more than ever. I've finally grasped the importance of enjoying my life, not just my calling, and I don't have my wife here to share it. Keep God first, but remember your wife should never have to compete for your time."

"Okay, Pastor." Timothy nodded in agreement. "I found a new chess opponent. A young guy fresh off the streets trying to find his way."

"Aren't we all?" Ananias studied his next move. "My pastor, Fred T. Williamson, started Gethsemane just after World War II. He thought that the Garden of Gethsemane was the most powerful passage in the entire Bible. To imagine our Lord and Savior in a place where he could identify with the struggles of humanity; the challenge to believe God and follow Him even when the road seemed impossible and the glimmer of hope seemed dim. I find it interesting how the Garden of Gethsemane must precede the resurrection."

Ananias moved another piece before he pointed at Timothy. "You have to remember that the people who pass through our doors are in their own personal Gethsemane. It's your job to point them to the resurrection." Ananias glanced up and noticed that Timothy had not taken his eyes off of him the entire time.

"You're a mighty man of God. I wouldn't have given my ministry to anyone less. The only thing I wish is that you were a better preacher."

"A better preacher? I have my own unique style."

"That puts people to sleep. Get some passion and fire behind those sermons."

"I distinctly remember you saying that you do not want someone to just entertain the crowd."

"I did, and I also don't want someone to bore the crowd either. The gospel is the good news."

"I would like to continue this verbal assault on my already fragile ego, but I have to go." Timothy looked at his watch and then made his final move. "That, I believe, is check and mate."

"I let you win," a baffled Ananias said.

Timothy stood up and headed for the door, but the evening felt incomplete for Ananias without some closure.

"So what are you going to do about Dennis?"

"I'm not going to sit him down, but I am going to recommend some marital counseling for him and his wife."

Not too long after Timothy left, Ananias got up and grabbed his large-print Bible. He opened it and turned to Hebrews 4:15. Before his heart attack, Ananias had planned to preach from this sermon.

He read the passage, and it compelled him to stand up and pretend that he was in front of the congregation.

"For we are not without a High Priest who can not be touched with the infirmities; but was in all points tempted but did not sin. Let us therefore come boldly unto the throne of grace, that we may obtain mercy, and find grace to help in time of need.

"Now, whatever you're going through, know this: you are not going through it alone. There is a High Priest who is willing to walk with you and show you how to defeat your enemies. How to tear down your strongholds. How to speak to your mountains and watch them move. Oh, Hallelujah. Praise Jesus."

CHAPTER TWENTY-EIGHT

Renee had not been to church since Dennis told her about the incident with Cecilia. She knew she was being talked about and laughed at behind her back. Her husband caused her too much embarrassment.

In the master bedroom, Renee heard Dennis come in and slam the door. The children were at her mother's house, so she did not worry about the abrasive entrance.

Curiosity caused Renee to get up and unlock the bedroom door. From a corner angle, she watched Dennis enter the kitchen and open the refrigerator. He came out with a carton of orange juice and began to drink without a cup. He turned around and Renee stood in the doorway. The moonlight through the window illuminated Dennis's eyes.

"Where are you coming from?" Renee asked.

"Church."

Renee could not even believe that he had been to church. His actions caused her to question everything about her husband.

"What were you doing there?"

"I had a meeting with Timothy."

"About what?"

"What do you think?"

"Don't get snappy with me!"

"It was about what happened. Timothy was the person I called for help when I left."

"I know you did, but I still don't understand why you would call him."

"Because I was too ashamed to call anyone else."

Renee walked over to the love seat and sat down Indian-style. "What did he suggest?"

"He didn't want to sit me down." Dennis sat on the couch adjacent to Renee.

"That's good, I guess."

"He suggested you and I go to marriage counseling."

Renee threw her arms in the air and let them fall as she flopped down onto the couch. "All he does is judge other folks like his life is perfect. That's why I can't stand him."

A few moments passed with only grunts between Renee and Dennis.

"So do you want to work on your marriage?" Renee asked.

"I don't know if I can. I know I've hurt you really bad."

"No, you don't know. You humiliated me."

"I'm sorry, I love—"

Renee put her hand up to stop Dennis. "Save it, because I don't believe you."

"But I do!"

"You don't love me enough if you cheated on me with another woman."

"That's not true."

"It's not? Then tell me how you can love someone and hurt them as bad as you hurt me."

Dennis did not respond, and by now, Renee was so filled with rage that she started to shake.

"Are you going to leave me with the kids?" Renee asked.

"I don't want to."

"Are you in love with her?"

"No!"

Renee jumped up with her hands on her hips. "That's what I can't understand about you men. You'll throw away a good thing for a woman you don't even love. You could've come to me."

"When?" Dennis stood up. "When would be a good time for me to talk to you about my issues, since we both seemed to be so wrapped up in making me pastor? The truth is I had no business trying be a pastor of my own church."

"Don't act like I forced you to become an ordained minister."

"You're right, you didn't, but you can't tell me that you didn't want to be First Lady."

"Here you go—don't want to man up to your own responsibilities, just want to shift the blame somewhere else."

"I'm not shifting the blame." Dennis walked around the coffee table and came within inches of Renee. "But I saw your reaction three years ago when you found out that Deacon Thomas was addicted to pornography and left the church. The truth is that I'm not the husband you brag about. I'm flawed, and I'm a hypocrite."

Renee walked over to Dennis. She looked him up and down before she gave him a light poke in the chest. "You're not a hypocrite; you're stronger than what you give yourself credit for. And up until last week, I was proud to be your wife. You broke my heart, Dennis, and I'm trying to put it back together so I can love you the way I want to, but I can't. I can't get past you being with another woman."

Renee covered her face to hide her tears, and Dennis gave her a hug and a kiss on her forehead. Renee did not fight the hug.

"I'm so sorry, baby," Dennis apologized sincerely.

Renee lifted her head from her hands and broke away from the hug.

"Ever since you told me that you cheated on me, I've been torn about whether or not to forgive you. I deserve better. I deserve someone who would treat me the way I deserve to be treated, because I'm a good woman and you're on the verge of losing me."

Renee walked to the bedroom, but before she went in, she turned around and looked at Dennis. "And I don't know if you can stay here while I try to figure things out."

She slammed the door and locked it. She did not respond to Dennis's repetitious knocks or pleas to unlock the door. Instead, Renee lay on the bed and cried herself to sleep.

Emerald thought she had come home to the wrong house. The lights were turned off and candles were lit throughout both the living and dining room. The room smelled of cinnamon. She felt a weird traction under her shoes and noticed that rose petals led to the middle of the living room.

"It's about time you got home." Timothy wore a black pinstripe shirt with black slacks.

"What's all this?" Emerald tossed her purse onto the couch.

"A break from the ordinary."

Timothy took Emerald by the hand and led her to the dining room with a white tablecloth spread out over the glass table and dinner for two on top. It was her favorite, salmon with vegetables.

"You made my favorite."

"The restaurant made your favorite. I just went and picked it up and put it on a plate."

Emerald and Timothy sat and ate. She savored every bite.

"This is really nice," Emerald complimented.

"I just want you to know that I love you, and I appreciate you standing by me this whole time."

"That's what I promised to do."

"This has been the most challenging thing I've ever done, and I couldn't have done it without you."

"Baby, I love you, and as long as you're pursuing your dreams, you can count on at least one supporter."

"You truly are a virtuous woman."

"I have to apologize. All this talk about quality time and kids, I mean, I didn't mean to put any more pressure on you, and I see now that you had a lot to deal with."

Timothy kissed Emerald before she could finish her sentence. Her senses went through the roof. His lips were coated in sincerity. She held his face, and her heart warmed to a degree that sent a sensation throughout her body.

There was no conversation about church. No cell phone interruption. Miles Davis played in the background as the candles burned, and Emerald went to sleep in her husband's embrace.

CHAPTER TWENTY-NINE

Timothy's day began at 4:36 AM with a phrase burned into his head: "A High Priest." Timothy sat up in his bed.

"What's wrong, babe?" Emerald asked, half-asleep.

"Nothing. Go back to sleep." Timothy tossed back the covers.

Timothy felt his way through the darkness to the living room. He turned on the lamp on the opposite side of his couch. It gave off enough light for Timothy to locate both his Bible and his concordance on the bookshelf. He set the books on the coffee table and grabbed a note tablet.

"Priest, priest!" He thumbed through the concordance.

Timothy found the word "priest" and scanned through the abbreviated books of the Bible. He came to the book of Hebrews and found the first part of the scripture.

"We are not without a high priest," Timothy said in a whisper.

After he read the scripture, Timothy's sermon came to him all at once.

He wrote until his hand started to ache and dawn emerged.

"Thank you, Jesus, for this awesome Word."

* * *

When Timothy arrived at church, Darius greeted him in a navy blue security jacket.

"What's good with you, Pastor?"

"I'm great. I got a Word today. How's everything with you?"

"Everything is good. I go in to serve my one year tomorrow, and I'm ready to go through this test so I can move on with my life."

"The Lord is going to see you through this."

"No doubt. Let me get that for you," Darius said, pointing to Timothy's briefcase.

"Why, thank you." Timothy handed his briefcase to Darius.

Timothy and Darius walked up the church steps and into the lobby. They passed by the greeters and some of the members.

"Glad to see you helping out," Timothy said to Darius.

"You know, God's blessings are tied up in service," Darius replied.

They arrived at Timothy's office, and Darius handed Timothy his briefcase.

"You need anything else?"

"No, thank you, sir."

Darius closed the door behind him and Timothy unpacked his bag. He removed a blue leatherbound Bible and yellow note tablet with lots of scribbled notes on it. Emerald walked into Timothy's office without so much as a knock. She had coffee in hand, and Timothy's ear caught a bit of the praise and worship music.

"Baby, I'm sorry, but I'm running late. Here's your coffee." Emerald set the coffee on Timothy's desk.

"Thanks, babe." Timothy took a sip from his coffee and continued to write notes.

He sipped coffee and wrote illustrations for several points. He'd left the DO NOT KNOCK sign on the outside door, so he was concerned when there was a sudden knock on the door. "Enter!" he called out.

Ananias poked his head in through the door. "Good morning, sir!"

"It's good to see you, Pastor." Timothy stood and shook Ananias's hand before returning to his seat.

"I figured I'd stop by and see if you needed a hand with anything."

"I'm good at the moment. I'll be preaching from Hebrews 4:11."

Ananias's eyes got big. "Well, if you need help in closing it out, you can just hand it over to me and I'll finish."

"You just sit back and enjoy. I can take it from here."

Ananias paced his old office and admired his awards and recognitions that still decorated the wall. "You didn't change the office much," he noted.

"That's because it constantly reminds me that I'm here because I stood on the shoulders of greatness."

Timothy could hardly contain himself. The music brought the congregation to their feet. Neither Dennis nor Renee attended service. Quincy filled in on the organ and brought his friend, Jamal, to cover the drums.

"Praise the Lord, saints," Timothy said.

"Praise the Lord," the church repeated.

The musicians ceased playing.

"Go ahead and keep playing," Timothy ordered them.

Quincy looked at Jamal, and they played again.

"We're going to take it back to the old school. Y'all remember old school church?" Timothy held up his hand and the church nodded in approval. "I remember when I was growing up and we would have old school services and we would be clapping our hands, and all of a sudden the organ would stop."

Quincy stopped the organ.

"Then the guitar would cut off."

Fred stopped the guitar.

"All that was left was the sound of us clapping."

The whole congregation clapped in a perfect cadence.

"Then the guitar would come back in."

Fred started to play again.

"Then the organ."

Quincy played the organ, and people in the congregation started to shout. Some people ran into the aisle. One lady danced in the middle of the pew, but an usher came over to assist her and keep her from injuring anyone else.

"We'll be here all day, but the Word of God must be preached."

The musicians stopped and Timothy opened his Bible. He did a quick scan around the sanctuary and saw Constance in the audience.

"The scripture reads: 'We are not without a high priest that is unable to sympathize with our weaknesses'—and the church said amen."

"Amen," the congregation replied.

"I want to do something a little different today. I want you to grab someone by the hand. You don't know what your neighbor is going through, but as we touch and agree right now, we're going to pray for one another and pray that God will intercede on our behalf."

The congregation stood up and people grabbed each other by the hand.

"Father, in the name of Jesus. All of you and none of me, Lord, as your servant brings forth this message. In Jesus' name, amen."

When Timothy concluded his prayer, Vernon and Kristal walked in. Vernon held Autumn's hand.

"When you become a Christian, it shouldn't take you long to realize that the true test of your faith occurs outside of these walls."

Timothy received more head nods than amens.

"When I read this scripture, I am filled with hope because I know that no matter what I go through, I have a High Priest who understands. In fact, we see in the garden of Gethsemane that Jesus Himself struggled with his flesh to do the will of God."

The amens came more frequently.

"But nevertheless, Jesus remained obedient, and because of Him, we not only have forgiveness of our sins, but we have someone in our corner who has overcome the world and is willing to teach us how to overcome our circumstances."

Some of the congregants jumped to their feet like firecrackers. People shuddered and cried. Amens and shouts filled the room.

"If you take away only one thing from this message, know that Jesus loves you and that you're worth going to the cross for and He desires to have a relationship with you. He wants to take away the pain. He wants to take away the fear and fill you with joy. He wants you to spend eternity with Him. Child of God, if you can get this in your spirit, then it won't matter what anyone has to say."

More people shot up out of their seats.

"That's why we come to church—to worship God, but also to be reminded that we're not alone in this fight, and if we're going to make it, we're going to make it together."

The majority of the congregants stood on their feet and the musicians started to play.

"It's not too late. It's not too late. Don't you leave here today thinking that it's too late! Jesus has already forgiven you; you just have to receive it. Why don't you come to this altar, and let's get back in line with God's will?"

Within moments, the altar overflowed with people. Kristal went to the altar while Vernon remained to watch his sister. Tina, a soloist at Gethsemane, got up and started to sing. Soon, Constance joined her and sang with tears in her eyes.

Timothy reveled in every second of it all.

"To God be the glory," Timothy proclaimed.

Timothy looked to his left and saw Emerald in tears with a smile. Ananias stood up next to Emerald with a big smile on his face. All he could do was wink at Timothy.

That day was a beginning of a journey for both Timothy and Ananias. Timothy's journey was to become a pastor, and Ananias's journey was to step aside and allow God to continue His work through Timothy. The people who attended services that day came in search of a redeemer and not a sermon. They found God and not man.

EPILOGUE

The graffiti on the walls and sidewalks resembled crayon colors in the daylight. Darius walked along the streets with a stack of invitations. His friend he had met in jail, Roberto, walked right beside him with his own stack of invitations in his hands.

"Man, I remember one time I was running from the po-po over here and got caught in the fence right over there." Roberto pointed to a gate between two apartments.

"Yeah, I think I've been over here once or twice," Darius stated.

They approached a block where some young hustlers hung out but not much traffic occurred. Darius could tell that this was not a hot spot and that none of the hustlers made any real money. They were not alert, and if it weren't for the occasional hand-to-hand action, Darius would have thought that they just hung out on the block for the heck of it.

"We got to get these cats saved, because they ain't getting no money," Darius said.

The second tallest boy had cornrows and put his hands in

his jacket pocket at the sight of Darius and Roberto. The shortest one gave Darius a pleasant head nod.

"What's good with you?" Darius asked.

"Nothing, man, just on the grind."

"I see, no doubt."

"So what's up? Y'all moving?"

"Naw, I just came to holla at you about something."

Darius and Roberto handed each boy an invitation.

"We want to invite y'all to our church," Roberto said.

"Fam, I thought y'all were about business," the tall boy with the cornrows said.

"Oh, we're about business all right. We're about our Father's business, God's business. I'm Darius, and this is my man, Roberto."

Darius and Roberto exchanged handshakes with the boys.

"I see you out here getting it, but check this out: how long you been on the block?" Darius asked.

"Like a year!" the boy with cornrows said.

"And in that time, how many of your people have you seen locked up or shot?"

"Too many," the young man said with a deep sigh.

"I'm saying, though, the streets is a trap designed to get us locked up or shot up, and for what?" Darius said.

"You know what? I can't speak on all preachers, but our pastor, he's a real dude, and he's serious about trying to help people," Roberto said.

"That's real spit right there," Darius said with a head nod. "Look, I was out here like y'all, getting it in, but then I almost lost my life to the game. I'm in my twenties and there's so much more to live for. Y'all younger than me. You probably don't even have a record. You could quit the game right now and wouldn't have to stress over being caught in the system," Darius said.

Even the dope fiends stood at attention; they hung onto Darius's every word.

"But let me get out of here, fam. Real talk, though. Come by the church, because God is doing some great things that I can't explain, but I guarantee you, you'll experience," Darius said.

"All right, fam. Stay up," the tall boy said.

Darius and Roberto exchanged pounds with all four boys. Darius walked back to his car and was overwhelmed with a sense of fulfillment. "It feels so good every time we come out here. It's rare to find someone who has a heart for witnessing. Let's grab some lunch," Darius said.

"That's what's up."

The mall was quiet with very little foot traffic, but Constance reveled in every moment. She sat at her table, took in the fresh air, and took sips from her iced tea. Quest's Bookstore not only had a plethora of books, but they also had a pretty substantial multimedia center. Constance grew emotional at the sight of the cover of the book in front of her. It had a picture of a woman with her back turned, gazing out into the ocean. On top, written in cursive in violet blue, was the title, *Virtuous Woman,* and on bottom was the author's name, Constance Anderson.

In light of her album being shelved, her journal was therapeutic. While reading some of her entries, she discovered that a lot of her thoughts and emotions would be very helpful to other young women. What started as journal entries turned into a book to guide women through tumultuous periods in their lives and reaffirm the need to have a relationship with God.

"Ms. Anderson?"

Constance put the book down. She turned to see a young girl in her early twenties with a copy of the book in her hands. The girl had olive skin and braids.

"Hello," Constance replied.

The girl handed Constance a copy of the book, and she turned to the title page with her pen in hand.

"Your book saved my life. Will you please autograph a copy for me?"

"Praise God," Constance said.

"I went through a bad break-up where my boyfriend at the time made me feel ugly and worthless. I didn't know who to talk to, because all of my family and friends were waiting to give me the 'I told you so' speech. So I suffered in silence."

Constance could feel the negative energy that this young girl felt; emotions that Constance had not felt in a long time.

"I know that must've been horrible."

"It was. It got so bad to the point where I thought about killing myself, but then I saw you on TV giving your testimony, and I was so touched that I ran to the bookstore and ordered a copy of your book."

A rush of joy and excitement overcame Constance because she knew that the girl's story was going to get better.

"I went through the whole book in a day, and afterwards, I felt so empowered. I just want to say thank you."

Constance pulled out tissue to wipe the tears from her eyes before they ruined her makeup. "You are so beautiful, my sister, and just like my story has been an inspiration to you, you've been an inspiration to me." Constance finished signing the book and handed it to the young girl.

"Thank you!"

"No, thank you." Constance stood up and gave the girl a hug.

The girl left, and though Constance did not sell a lot of books at this particular book signing, she felt like the event was more than successful. The same way God had used her to touch that young girl's life, God had used the young girl to touch hers and remind her that her life, her pain, her heartache, and her struggles had not been in vain.

* * *

"How have you been sleeping?" Dr. Goethe asked.

Vernon lifted his head up with a big smile and eyes full of joy.

"I haven't had any nightmares," Vernon told his therapist.

"That's excellent news."

"My pastor has been spending a lot of time with me, encouraging me to get involved in sports. I'm going to go out for the soccer team next year."

"Soccer? That's great."

"There's also this guy that takes me to the movies. Darius. He's real cool."

"It sounds like you really enjoy going to church."

"Sometimes I don't want to leave."

Dr. Goethe leaned forward and pushed his glasses back. "Vernon, you have survived a horrendous ordeal. Now, you don't have to cover up anything in here. You're free to be honest, okay?"

"This girl in my class, Rachael, she passed me a note the other day saying that she thought I was cute."

"And how do you feel about Rachael?"

"I don't know. Okay, I guess."

"You're only thirteen. Don't put too much pressure on yourself." Dr. Goethe looked at his watch. "Time's up."

"See you next time, Dr. Goethe." Vernon grabbed his backpack and walked out.

On the other side of the door was Kristal. She had a bag of food and a soft drink in one hand.

"How did it go, baby?" Kristal asked.

"It went okay."

Kristal rubbed Vernon's head. Vernon looked at his mother and she smiled.

"Come on. Let's go get your sister."

Vernon was excited about today. His mother was going to take him and his sister to the beach and later to a movie.

Thanks to God, Vernon believed that he and his family were going to make it.

Dennis held on to Jasmine's hand, and Elijah walked alongside him. The three seemed to match, all wearing white suits. Jasmine had on her white dress with pink ribbons around her pigtails.

"What did you learn in Sunday school?" Dennis asked.

"We colored a picture of Noah and the Ark. Look, Daddy." Jasmine held out a picture with unique colors of animals, including lambs colored in orange. This image sparked a smile from Dennis. "That's lovely, sweetie."

"Dad, you coming to my game next Saturday?" Elijah asked.

"You bet. I don't plan to miss it."

Renee stood outside of the minivan with dark shades on. Dennis stopped in his tracks and kneeled down to Jasmine. "All right, sweetie. Daddy will see you soon."

Jasmine started to tear up. Dennis grabbed her and gave her a big hug, and a tear dropped from his eyes.

"Daddy, I want you to come home," Jasmine said.

"I will, sweetie. I promise."

Dennis let go of Jasmine and looked Elijah square in the eyes. "You continue to take care of your mother and your sister, you hear?"

Elijah nodded his head.

"I love you, son, and you're going to be a better man than I am. You hear me?"

Elijah nodded again and Dennis gave him a hug and a kiss on the cheek. The two children ran toward Renee. She stooped down and gave them a hug. She then slid the door back on the mini-van to let them in. Renee walked toward Dennis, and he stood up to meet her.

"Glad to see you found a church home," Renee said.

Dennis looked back at the sign on the front of the building that read: VICTORY TEMPLE.

"Yeah, it was hard to find a church home, but it's been good. I've just enjoyed coming and getting fed. I haven't played the organ yet or anything. What about you?"

"Still at Gethsemane teaching Sunday school. They made some changes that I feel are putting the church back on the right track. But a lot of members left as a result, including Constance."

"Wow," Dennis said in shock.

"You look good."

"I don't know how. I ain't been eating right."

They both shared a laugh, and then there was a moment of silence.

"I want to come home," Dennis stated.

"I don't know if I'm ready for you to." Renee brushed away some of her hair from her face.

"Renee, I love you, and I want us to be a family. You see how this is affecting the kids."

"I know, but I still need some time."

Dennis put his head down and turned away. He then turned back around and walked up to Renee and gave her a kiss on the cheek. He took her by the hand. "You're worth it. No matter how long it takes, I want us to be together."

Renee pulled back the hair that was blowing in the wind and placed it behind her ears.

"I haven't stopped loving you," Dennis said. "I love you so much, Renee, and I'm so sorry."

Renee walked to the car, and just as she was about to open the driver's side door, she turned around and looked at Dennis. "Maybe you can make me dinner on Friday."

"You know I don't cook."

"You got until Friday to learn how." Renee winked, got in the car, and then drove away.

Dennis stood there with a smile on his face, holding his Bible with joy.

* * *

New Day Christian Center was established a year ago. Timothy decided that if he were to start a church, then he would want the church to be a place of new beginnings. New Day Christian Center was located in what used to be a hardware store near downtown San Jose.

It seated about 150, and every Sunday it was full to capacity as saints danced and shouted.

Timothy paced back and forth with his shoulders back as sweat poured from his brow. The congregation could not sit down as he shouted into the microphone.

"Don't let the devil talk you out of your destiny. If God said it, then surely it will come to pass."

The music started off in a wild staccato, and then settled into a rhythm that caused everyone to clap on beat. Timothy took a towel from his pulpit and wiped his face.

"There's someone here who wants to make Jesus their Lord and Savior. It doesn't matter what you have done; we've all fallen short of the grace of God, but if you come to this altar, I promise you that God will make it right."

The music settled into a soft melody, almost in a melancholy tone.

Constance got up and started to sing "Make Me Over Again." More people arrived at the altar. Kristal, in her usher uniform, directed them.

The song was so powerful that Timothy, who sat down at the beginning of the song, wanted to stand up, but his hands were glued to Emerald's perfectly shaped round stomach.

After service, Timothy walked back to his office, a much smaller space than his office at Gethsemane. He sat in the midst of pictures with politicians, special recognitions, his degrees, and pictures with his family. There was also a newspaper clipping with the headline *Beloved Pastor and Community Leader Dies at Age Sixty-five.*

The article went on to talk about the life of Pastor Ananias Jones and his contribution to his church and his community.

Timothy had done the eulogy at Ananias's funeral. In the months that followed his death, the board replaced Timothy with Pastor McClendon from Dallas, Texas, despite the fact that Timothy had managed to save the church from eviction.

At his desk with his hand balled into a half-closed fist over his mouth, Timothy stared at his open Bible, which had the passage of scripture from the Book of 2Timothy 2:20-21

> [20]*In a great house there are articles not only of gold and silver, but also of wood and clay; some are for noble purpose and some for ignoble.* [21]*If a man cleanses himself from the latter, he will be an instrument for noble purposes, made holy, useful to the Master and prepared to do any good work.*

A smile spread over Timothy's face because he now had his sermon for next week.

Reader's Group Guide Questions

1. Do you think that Constance should have told James that she was pregnant?

2. Did Renee overreact to Dennis kissing another woman?

3. Do you feel Ananias represented a dying breed of pastors?

4. Which person do you think had the most influence on Kristal's decision to change her life?

5. What type of impact do you believe Darius will have in ministry?

6. How do you think Vernon's experience will impact his faith?

7. Why do you think the board got rid of Timothy in the end?

8. What is the significance of the section entitled, "After the Benediction"?

9. What do you feel was the significance of the detailed description of Constance putting on makeup?

10. Which character's journey ministered to you the most?

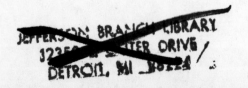